The Executive Producers

An Ella Graepenteck Genealogy Mystery

Erika Maren Steiger

E. STEIGER & CO.

LOS ANGELES

Published 2023 by E. Steiger & Co.
www.esteigerandco.com

ISBN: 978-1-951264-17-8

This is a work of fiction. Names, characters, places, and incidents are products of the author's imagination or are used fictitiously and are not to be construed as real. Any resemblance to actual events, locales, organizations, or persons, living or dead, is entirely coincidental.

Cover design by James, GoOnWrite.com

for my dear friend Maia Segura,

who has been impressing and inspiring me since the

day we met as teenagers on the verge of adventure,

and who has a jawdropping ability to make impossible

things happen

Contents

CHAPTER 1

Word of Mouth

It had to be in the house. There was nowhere else it could be.

I looked through every drawer, even the oddly small ones in the pantry, the ones I never use. I dragged out the stepladder to check the high shelves in the closets. No luck.

I was about to take a second pass at looking under the living room furniture when my stomach grumbled at me, insisting that I reevaluate my priorities. I had to admit that it was way past lunchtime, and my search process wasn't working anyway. Maybe a break and some food would jog my memory.

I put together some cheese and bread and mustard and sat at the kitchen counter, holding the sandwich in my left hand and scrolling through my phone with my right.

I had a voicemail.

I didn't recognize the number, but I went ahead and listened to it anyway. It would help pass the time, and I had a lot more sandwich to eat.

A deep voice, deliberate in its enunciation yet bouncing with urgency, claimed to be Detective Figueroa from LAPD Central Division, and said that Detective Roth from Hollywood Division had recommended me as a consultant. The voice recited a phone number, repeated it, and asked me to call.

It sounded real, not like a scam or a prank, but you can't always tell about those things, so I thought it prudent to check with Detective Roth, both to make sure he had indeed recommended me and to see if he could tell me why this Detective Figueroa was interested in my help.

I finished my sandwich, and I still hadn't thought of any new places to search, or had any revelatory memories of having put it somewhere unusual, so I decided to go ahead and make that call.

The afternoon sun had reached a sharp angle through the kitchen window, which was probably why I could feel my cheeks getting warmer as I picked up my phone, found Cormac Roth in my contacts, and then reached toward the button with the anachronistic little telephone receiver on it. I find it amusing that young people who have never in their lives picked up an actual telephone receiver, nor are likely ever to do so, will always associate a pictograph of one with making or receiving a call. Every time I touch that little button I experience a small stab of enjoyment of that fact. Sometimes it is mixed with mild nostalgia for the days of holding that big plastic thing to my ear and twirling the curly cord around my fingers as I talked.

As my finger hovered over the button, it occurred to me that perhaps I should call him on his work line. This was, after all, a business call. It was a casual question though, did he recommend me or not, and I didn't want to make too much of it, and since our communication lately had all been on his personal number, it might seem strange not to use it. I went with the personal number.

He picked up on the first ring, which wasn't necessarily indicative of anything, but which my ego took as a compliment nonetheless. The enthusiasm of his initial "Hi!" encouraged my ego's interpretation. Cormac and I established that we were both doing fine, and then I jumped right into the purpose for my call.

"I'm actually calling primarily for a business reason."

"Oh." Did he sound disappointed? Maybe a little.

"I heard from a Detective Figueroa. He said you recommended me."

"Yeah I did. He needs some genealogy research."

"I wanted to make sure it was a real thing."

"Oh. Yeah. He's a good guy, and a good detective. I've known him since the academy."

"Great! Then I'll call him and tell him I'll do it."

"Good. Yeah. I told him you'd be great, you're the best."

"Thanks. That was nice of you."

"Yeah. I mean, no problem. It's the truth."

"Thanks."

"Yeah. Sure. You're welcome."

"All right then."

"Yeah."

"So I guess I'll call him."

"Yeah. Oh you mean now."

"I guess, unless there's something else."

"No. I mean, if you don't have anything else."

"Nothing important."

"Yeah."

"Okay. I'll talk to you soon then."

"Yeah."

"Okay."

"Yeah, um, hey Ella?"

"Yes?"

"If you're not busy Saturday, let's do something."

"Sure, yes, I'd like that."

"Okay, good. We'll figure out details later."

"Sure."

"Yeah."

"I guess I'll go call that detective now."

"Yeah."

"Bye."

"Bye."

I looked at my calendar, to make sure I hadn't forgotten that I already had something scheduled on Saturday. I hadn't. It was clear.

The conversation tried to replay itself in my head, to dwell on the embarrassing possibility that some of the things I said might have sounded stupid, or on the positive side, to build anticipation for the upcoming date, but I cut it off. I had no time or patience for annoying feelings. I had work to do.

I listened to that voicemail again, to refresh my memory about exactly what Detective Figueroa had said, and to make sure I had gotten his phone number into my contacts correctly.

He picked up on the second ring.

"Figueroa."

"Hello Detective Figueroa. This is Ella Graepenteck. You left me a voicemail."

"Right! The consultant, the genealogist. Thanks for getting back to me. I appreciate it."

"No problem. How can I help you?"

"Immediately down to business. That's good. I like that. So, I've got a murder investigation, just started, real early stages, and one thing that's a little unusual, that definitely looks like a lead, is the victim had a note on her, a piece of paper, folded up in a pocket, and it says, 'I know about your family' on it."

"Wow."

"Right, and that could mean a lot of things, but nothing stands out as the obvious thing, from what we know so far. We haven't found any skeletons in the closet, or anything like that, and the family says they have no idea what it could be, no secrets they're hiding, so it seems like some research on the subject could be important, really help the investigation."

"Absolutely."

"Right, so I thought I should find an expert on that sort of thing, someone who does this kind of research, who knows what to look for, so I asked around, and Detective Roth said he knew the perfect person, the exact right one for the job, and that was you."

"Well, I hope I'll be able to help you with your investigation. I can certainly research the family for you."

"Terrific! Right. So, how do we get going? What information do you need from me? How can I help you with your work?"

"All I need to get started are all the names and birthdates you know of, for all the family members."

"I've got that info for the victim and her parents and her sisters, all the immediate family."

"That's a great start. Does the police department need anything from me? When I worked with Detective Roth I had to fill out some paperwork, to become an official consultant. Do you know if I have to do that again for your division?"

"I don't think so. I think I just request to work with you. I think it transfers over."

"Maybe I should check with the administrator who approved it originally, just to be certain."

"That's probably a good idea. Might as well make sure. Get all the ducks in a row."

He gave me all the family names and birthdates, then filled me in on the basics of the case, and that was it. We hung up.

Next I called Melanie Browning, at Hollywood Division. My recollection of her was that she had welcomed my presence with the warmth most people would reserve for an infestation of termites, but she was responsible and efficient when it came to doing her job. I had no doubt she would be as helpful as professionally necessary.

"Melanie Browning."

"Hello. This is Ella Graepenteck, the genealogist? You helped me get my official status as a consultant with the department."

She was quiet for several seconds, but then I heard the cool politeness I remembered, including the oddly staccato way she pronounced my name. It was correct and yet, somehow, not quite right.

"Yes, of course, Ms. grape-in-teck."

"I've been asked to work with Detective Figueroa, in Central Division, and I just wanted to know if there are any additional forms I have to fill out or steps I have to take."

"In Central Division? I see. How nice that you're working with the department again. There are no additional forms for you, until you are requesting payment. You remember the form for that?"

"Yes. So I'll just need Detective Figueroa to sign that when we're done?"

"That's correct. You can go right ahead and get to work."

"All right then. Thank you very much for your help."

"You're welcome. Best of luck in your work with Central Division!" Did she sound a little excited that I would be working with a detective in a different division? Maybe it was my imagination.

"Thanks."

After I hung up I remembered that I still hadn't found it, which was frustrating. It shouldn't be that hard to find. Any light would glint off its golden surface, especially when the little wheels moved, and it couldn't have gone far. It absolutely had to be somewhere in the house, but further searching would just have to wait. I had a murder to help solve.

CHAPTER 2

Connections

The murder victim had been found on Olvera Street, the partially restored, partially recreated vestige of the Spanish colonial era that is very popular with tourists. Its official name is El Pueblo Historic Park, and it bills itself as "the birthplace of Los Angeles". It's downtown, near Union Station, and across the 101 freeway from a lot of city government and courthouse buildings. I've had jury duty in the area a couple of times. Aside from lunchbreaks on those occasions, my principal experiences of Olvera Street were as a kid, on school field trips. I remember dancers in bright colors, festive mariachi music, and tasty food, mostly tacos and taquitos. A dead body there did not fit at all with the general tone of the place. It tended to be crowded too. I found it hard to imagine someone could have been killed there without any witnesses, but so far none had come forward.

Detective Figueroa had told me they were trying to keep the identity of the victim from becoming public for as long as possible, because they were afraid fans might disrupt the crime scene, or otherwise make investigation difficult. The reason fans might be a problem was that the victim was Hannah Chao, the youngest of the three sisters who made up the former pop group Brite, which had a couple of big hits about ten years ago.

Curiosity led me to look for old interviews and other information about the group. I was the 14,679,802nd person to view a video of them performing their biggest hit, unimaginatively entitled "I Love U", at one of those trendy, expensive music festivals. They wore jeans and faux leather jackets and boots, identical except for color. Hannah was in yellow, eldest sister Nina in red, and middle sister Olivia in blue. It was unclear if their choice of the primary colors had any significance. I didn't find them wearing that particular assortment of colors in any other performances.

They danced a few simple steps and executed some fairly effective harmonies. They were reasonably good singers. Hannah was very young in the video. I would guess she was 14, maybe 15 at the oldest. It was disconcerting to think of her as already dead. Her main functions in the group seemed to be looking cute and being enthusiastic. The star of the band was clearly Nina. In addition to being the eldest, she sang most of the melody lines, and she was wearing bright red, but she gave the impression that she would be the one who drew the focus even without those things. She had a compelling stage presence, significantly outshining her sisters.

A little more online exploring showed me that the Chao sisters did still have a relatively small but devout core group of fans. They called themselves Briters and spent a lot of time discussing the group on social media. I thought I might look into that more later, but first I had some fundamental work to do.

I went to my favorite genealogy website and created a new family tree with Hannah Chao as the starting point. I added her parents, Edward and Christina, and her sisters, Nina and Olivia, and then started looking for information to add.

The grandparents were easy to find. Edward Chao's parents were Robert Chao and June Wallace. They were born in the late 1930s and married in Los Angeles in 1957. Christina Morales Chao's parents were David Morales and Rose Kahale. They were born a few years later than Robert and June and married in Los Angeles in 1959.

Some of the great grandparents popped right up too. David Morales' parents were Daniel Morales and Anna Jones. Robert Chao's parents were Albert Chao and Catherine Ming. Both couples had been married in Los Angeles in the 1930s.

Once I had the basic tree established, I went back to my internet explorations.

The first interview of Brite that I came across was from that same music festival. The sisters were still in their primary color outfits. After a few introductory questions about how exciting it was to be there and how welcoming the audience was, the topic moved briefly, but helpfully for me, to their ancestry. I wasn't surprised that Nina did most of the talking.

"How do you feel about representing the Asian American community?"

"We are proud to be part of the Asian American and Pacific Islander community, and we hope the community is proud of us, that they consider us positive representatives. We are also proud of all the other parts of our family. Most people know about our Chinese heritage, but we also have Hawaiian, and Mexican, and African, and lots of other things. We are very multicultural, and we are proud of that."

"You have Hawaiian heritage?"

"Yes, our grandmother is Hawaiian."

"Do you know how to dance the hula?"

"Well, Hawaiian culture is more than just hula."

"Oh yeah, of course. No offense meant."

"Mmhmm."

"So, I understand you are working on a new album."

In just about every interview I found, they stated how proud they were to be multicultural, and they almost always specifically mentioned their Hawaiian grandmother. I figured that must be Rose Kahale, Christina Morales Chao's mother. They often talked about how supportive she was of their music career. It seemed they were very close to her. Nina also frequently said it made them feel very American, and very Californian, to have ancestors of so many different racial and ethnic backgrounds. The phrases she used, like that bit about being proud to be part of the community and hoping the community was proud, were impressively consistent, clearly the result of training by a professional. Brite must have had a publicist.

The sisters, usually Nina, but occasionally Olivia or Hannah, also often discussed their Chao ancestral line. Apparently the Chaos had immigrated from China quite a few generations back, first working in restaurants and then saving up enough to purchase one of their own, and eventually owning several. It was the revenue from those restaurants that had paid for the sisters' singing and dancing lessons, and for the recording of demos. It was a fairly standard American Dream rags to riches story, and one that Brite, or at least whoever managed their publicity, seemed keen to promote.

I decided to look into what the fans, the Briters, were talking about these days. They didn't seem to have discovered yet that Hannah had been killed. The main topic of discussion was that Nina, who was apparently trying to build a career as an actress, had scored an important supporting role in a new big budget studio film. It seemed Hannah was working with her, or for her, helping her with her acting ambitions. There was very little discussion of middle sister Olivia, and what there was mostly centered around questions about what she was up to, and speculation that she had quit the entertainment business for good.

I was curious about Nina's movie role, especially because if Hannah had been a sort of employee of hers, she was probably involved in the production in some way, likely as Nina's assistant, or something similar. The film was called Sterling, and a quick search told me that it was about 1920s socialite Christine Sterling, who, among other things, was a major force in the original creation of the tourist hotspot known as Olvera Street.

Interesting.

I decided to find out more about this movie. It wasn't hard to find a few stories about it. The studio seemed to be positioning it as one of their biggest films of the year. There were mentions of it in lots of places, including major news outlets, not just gossip sites and entertainment blogs. I was surprised I hadn't heard of it before.

The production was just getting started filming in Los Angeles, both in the studio and on location, and Olvera Street was one of the planned locations. I wouldn't expect the producers would be happy about its now being a crime scene. That would undoubtedly cause some very expensive delays.

One of the entertainment industry publications had a detailed story that listed some of the actors.

Oscar winner Stephanie Warrick stars as Christine Sterling, leading an impressive cast including Oscar nominee Jack Laraby, Instagram favorite Anthony Kells, and up and comer Nina Chao. Filming is scheduled for the next four months, with a release date planned near the end of next year.

At the end of the article was a list of the executive producers. It was a long list, as is frequently the case. The title executive producer doesn't necessarily imply any actual interaction with the production of a movie or a television show. What it does imply is financial involvement, and ego enhancement, sometimes one or the other and sometimes both. I didn't expect to be familiar with the names, as I don't make a point of keeping up on the intricacies of the film industry, but I skimmed through them anyway.

I was glad no one was in the room with me as I perused the list, because pretty soon I heard myself spit out the words "Oh crap!" and the abruptness and the volume of the words would have startled and perhaps frightened anyone who had been there, as would the sight of me throwing a notebook and pen that happened to be near my right hand. I only threw them across the bed, and I wasn't out of control enough to throw the computer, but the sentiment did seem to require some form of physical expression. My actions were absolutely justified, but still, I was happy that there was no one there to observe my behavior.

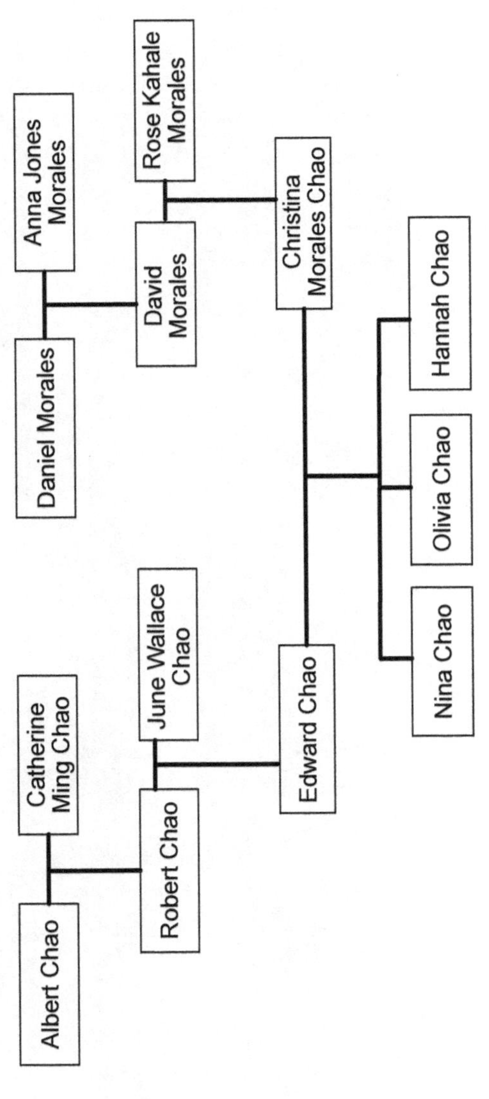

Anna Jones Morales
Rose Kahale Morales
Daniel Morales
David Morales
Christina Morales Chao
Catherine Ming Chao
June Wallace Chao
Albert Chao
Robert Chao
Edward Chao
Nina Chao
Olivia Chao
Hannah Chao

CHAPTER 3

Olvera Street

Among the fifteen or so names on that list of executive producers, quite near the top, was the one that caused my embarrassing outburst: Nicholas de Brisay III.

He is my cousin, more precisely my second cousin once removed. His grandfather, Nicholas de Brisay, was one of the many sons of Patrick de Brisay Jr. The eldest of those sons, Patrick de Brisay III, was my mother's grandfather, which means Nicholas de Brisay III's father, Nicholas de Brisay Jr., was first cousin to my mother's father, Patrick de Brisay IV.

The de Brisays have not, as a rule, been very creative in naming their children, especially the boys, which makes sorting them out confusing. It's something a descendant, especially a genealogist, simply has to get used to. The upshot is, Nicholas de Brisay III and my mother are second cousins, making me his second cousin once removed.

My mother and I are the only living members of her branch of the de Brisay family, the descendants of Patrick de Brisay III, and we've never had much to do with any of the other branches. They can be hard to like, and even harder to respect, unless you like and respect people according to how much wealth they control and how much power they wield, in which case there are some de Brisays you would positively adore. One of the favorite pastimes of many of them is throwing large sums of money around, sometimes as straightforward gambling, in places such as Las Vegas, and sometimes as less obvious kinds of gambling, commonly referred to as investments, but usually, in either case, with the primary goal of drawing attention to themselves.

I wouldn't say I know Nicholas de Brisay III, although I might have met him once or twice, as a child. When my grandfather, Patrick de Brisay IV, was still alive, my mother and I used to attend the occasional big family event. Seeing that name on that list did cause my stomach to tighten a bit, both because it is uncomfortable in general to be reminded that I am connected to that family, and also because it occurred to me there could be conflict of interest issues in my being involved in this investigation.

I comforted myself with the fact that I had been hired only to research the family of Hannah Chao, and my second cousin once removed was not likely to be part of that. So, even if he and this film he was partially executive producing should come up in the investigation of the crime, they wouldn't be in my area of responsibility. Since Nicholas de Brisay III and my connection to him probably wouldn't matter at all, I decided to put him out of my mind and go back to researching the Chao family.

It was fairly easy to find more ancestors, but none of them showed any obvious indications of being the kind of ancestor one would want to keep secret. In fact, most of them seemed like the type most people would be proud to acknowledge as part of their history.

While I was still in the midst of discovering nothing of use, Detective Figueroa called.

"I'm going to take another look at the crime scene, check it over, make sure I didn't miss anything. I thought maybe you'd want to meet me there, provide another set of eyes."

"I absolutely would."

I got into my little blue Fiat and drove downtown. I had neglected to ask the detective from which end of Olvera Street I should enter, so I picked the end I preferred, the large plaza with the gazebo in the center, which often serves as a stage for performances. Although the promenade itself was completely blocked off, with a couple of uniformed officers standing guard, the plaza was populated with people enjoying the sunshine, and others avoiding it under the trees. Many from both groups were sneaking glances at the officers and then whispering intently. My choice of entrance was serendipitous, because Detective Figueroa was waiting for me with those two officers, who let us through and then kept any of the people watching from the plaza from following us.

I followed the detective down the right side of the brick walkway, between the center row of kiosks and the shops and restaurants on the eastern side, closest to Union Station. I had expected the place to feel smaller than I remembered, as is usual when returning to childhood haunts, but it didn't. That was probably because all the kiosks were locked up, many with metal bars across their doors, instead of overflowing with displays of dolls and masks and dresses for sale, allowing the walkway to feel much wider than it usually did. The relative bleakness and the quiet increased what had been to that point only a minimal sense of dread, focusing my thoughts on the fact that I was about to see the place where a dead body had been found.

The emerging sight of the Avila Adobe provided momentary distraction, its white walls and brown shutters contrasting with the bright colors of the kiosks. There was a sign by the staircase up to its high porch declaring it to be the oldest house in Los Angeles. I remembered going inside it, being impressed by its broad courtyard filled with fruit trees and birdsong, but it too was locked up now. We walked right past it.

Just beyond the house, on our right, was one of the larger restaurants, and to our left there was a break in the center row of kiosks, leaving room for several tall trees with expansive canopies, and creating a mini-plaza between that restaurant and another one over on the left side. The detective slowed his walk, so I knew we must be close.

He stopped as we approached a two-tiered fountain, painted a light blue very similar to the color of my car. The wall and the locked doors of the shop behind it were nearly the same color, making the fountain seem almost to disappear into them. There was a low brick wall topped with planters full of colorful flowers next to the fountain on the side facing us, and the rest of it was surrounded by two wide circular steps covered in rocks the size of cats.

The detective pointed at the ground in front of us.

"There. She hit her head on those rocks."

"Next to the fountain?"

"Right."

"So it could have been an accident."

"Maybe. She hit them pretty hard though."

"She was pushed."

"With considerable force, either by a strong person, or a very angry person."

"Or both."

"Right."

To keep from imagining too vividly what it would feel like to land on the rough edges of those rocks, I changed the subject.

"So, it turns out the Chao sisters had some interesting ancestors."

Detective Figueroa turned toward me and examined the expression on my face. It seemed he decided to indulge my avoidance technique, because his response was, "Really?"

"I don't know if I've found the ones we're looking for yet, but for example, Rose Kahale Morales, their maternal grandmother, came to Los Angeles from Honolulu by herself, at the age of 17."

"That was brave. Not everyone could do something like that."

"True. She seems to have been an impressive person. The sisters talked about her a lot in interviews, when they were popstars. She must have met David Morales, their grandfather, when they were both working in one of the big hotels here. He was a hotel manager."

"Oh yeah?"

"According to local directories of the time, yes. The Morales family had been in L.A. a long time, back at least to the era this place is designed to evoke."

"A couple hundred years, maybe?"

"Probably more. David's mother came here from Georgia though, by herself, at a young age, similar to what Rose did."

"Sounds like there were a lot of brave women in that family."

"It seems so. Her name was Anna Jones. It was probably controversial when she got married, in the 1930s, because she was Black, and Daniel Morales, David's father, wasn't."

"But that wouldn't be something to threaten the family over, not now."

"No. In fact, the sisters talked often in those interviews I saw about how proud they were of their multiracial heritage."

"So that's their mother's side of the family, right? What about their father's?"

"Their father's parents' marriage was probably controversial too. It was in 1957, if I remember correctly. The Chao family had been in the U.S. for many generations, but they seem to have always married other people of Chinese descent. Then Edward's father, Robert Chao, married June Wallace, who had no Chinese ancestry at all. She was born in New Hampshire, and her ancestors were most likely all from northern Europe."

"Did she come here alone too, like Rose and Anna?"

"No. Her parents moved here when she was a baby."

"So, nothing there the sisters would pay to keep quiet, either."

"Not that I have found so far."

Detective Figueroa walked forward a couple of paces and crouched down by the rocky steps. He looked around, taking in the view from that vantage point. Then he stood up and looked around again.

"This isn't a bad choice for a blackmail meeting point."

"Why's that?"

"The buildings around here would all be empty in the middle of the night, and they would block the view from farther away, so that reduces the possibility of witnesses. Also, there are lots of potential hiding places, between those kiosks, behind this wall, dark corners everywhere. If you wanted your victim to just drop the money and leave, you could watch them do it, without being seen."

"Makes sense. I've always wondered why a blackmailer would meet their victim in person. It seems awfully risky to let your blackmailee know who you are."

"Yeah, blackmail is a dangerous business."

"So if Hannah was the one being blackmailed, how did she end up murdered? Isn't it usually the blackmailer who turns up dead?"

"Right. It often goes that way. That's one of the strange things about this case."

"How do you know Hannah wasn't the blackmailer? Maybe she was the one who made the note, and she just hadn't given it to the person yet. Maybe she was blackmailing multiple people."

"All that's possible. It would fit the regular pattern better, be more what I would expect, but that note was all folded up in her pocket, more like one she'd received than one she was going to hand out, and she was famous, from a famous family."

"Which makes her a likely target for blackmail."

"And if she was seen she might get recognized, so that would make it hard to get away with it, if she was the perpetrator."

"Which brings us back to what you were saying about hiding. I just don't see why a blackmailer would kill someone who could still be a source of money. Maybe the blackmailer and the murderer were two different people."

"That could be too. A lot of scenarios are possible. We don't have a lot of leads though. Her being blackmailed about her family seems like the best one."

"Well, whoever killed her, there was a fight, right? And Hannah was pushed."

"Right. There were some small lacerations on Hannah's hands and arms, defensive wounds, no skin under her nails though."

"Maybe she hit her head before she had a chance to scratch the killer."

"That's probably it."

The detective did some more looking around, examining potential hiding places, looking at the fountain from different angles, and then announced that he had seen enough. I had no desire to stay there any longer, so we both went back to our cars.

When I returned home, I did some more research on the Chao family. I found a few more ancestors, but none that seemed like potential topics for blackmail. I also looked for more information about the ancestors I'd already found.

It was the sisters' paternal grandfather Robert Chao who had taken the one restaurant his parents owned and expanded the business into multiple locations. Internet searching uncovered several old local news articles about grand openings for new restaurants. One of the articles, from 1973, included a quotation from Robert about the chain's name:

My parents called their restaurant Chez Chao because they wanted to make it clear that it wasn't just an ordinary Chinese takeout place. We have always served a mix of traditional Chinese dishes and our own creations based on a variety of influences from all over the world. Chez Chao is the place to go for delicious food, both familiar favorites and new dishes to try.

It seemed that the multicultural bent emphasized in the interviews with Brite began in the Chao family several generations before the popstar sisters. Also, the ability to phrase things as a publicist would may have come to them naturally, even without careful training. Their grandfather obviously had a knack for it. Maybe it was passed down.

The articles were largely complimentary, emphasizing excitement about the new establishments. Most of them also provided the same rags to riches, American Dream narrative that the Brite interviews did. It seemed to have been a good marketing decision, in both cases, as the endeavors were successful both times.

So far, I had found nothing the Chao sisters would be likely to find the slightest bit embarrassing, not even as embarrassing as I found the de Brisays. There was no evidence yet of anything that would be a reason for someone to threaten them with the words, "I know about your family."

There had to be something, somewhere. I would just have to keep digging.

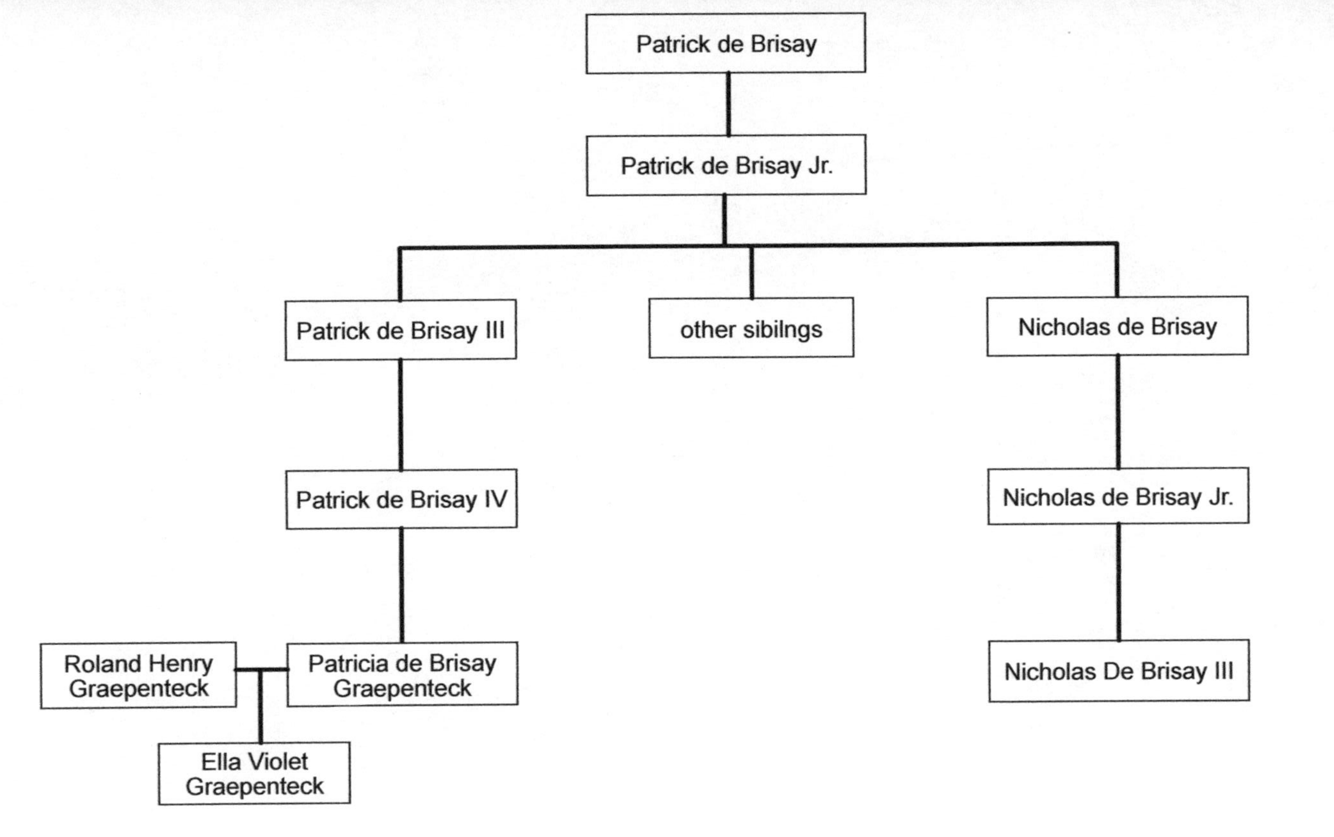

Patrick de Brisay
Patrick de Brisay Jr.
Patrick de Brisay III
other sibilngs
Nicholas de Brisay
Patrick de Brisay IV
Nicholas de Brisay Jr.
Roland Henry Graepenteck
Patricia de Brisay Graepenteck
Nicholas De Brisay III
Ella Violet Graepenteck

CHAPTER 4

Norwalk

Detective Figueroa hadn't given me any documentation for the Chao family birth information, just the names and dates they gave him, and while I didn't think it likely they had lied, I find, humans being what they are, it's always a good idea to confirm what they tell you. Relatively recent records like those aren't generally available online, and these weren't, but the Chao sisters, and their parents, as well as some of their grandparents, were all born in Los Angeles County, so I had an easy solution to that problem. As I had done many times before, I drove down to Norwalk to get documentation from the County Registrar-Recorder office.

I went after rush hour, so the traffic wasn't too bad. It took me less than an hour to go the 30 or so miles. The small parking lot was crowded as usual, but my little blue Fiat can slide into the tiny spaces bigger cars can't manage. As in most parking lots, there are always one or two SUVs or pickup trucks there whose drivers demonstrate their disdain for, or at least obliviousness to, the needs of other humans by parking way over the white line between spaces, making the next space essentially useless. Luckily for me, however, their thoughtlessness doesn't have much effect on people in tiny little cars.

I walked up the wide stairs in front of the building, weaving around all the people standing on them and chatting. I passed through the heavy glass doors, avoided the information desk and all the people huddled around it, and made it to the elevators, and from there down to the basement. I made a few familiar turns along dark, quiet hallways lined with boxes. One of these days I will remember to ask someone why there are always cardboard boxes piled up against the walls down there. I suspect it has something to do with available storage space, but there may be a far more interesting reason, and someday I will find out if there is. Finally, I walked into room 208.

Nadia Rodriguez was standing behind the front counter, placing papers into piles. Because of her height, she had to lean over in order to do so, and her perfectly straight, glossy black hair that, when she was fully vertical, must have just brushed her shoulders, fell down around her face.

"Nadia!"

She tried to keep a neutral expression, but she couldn't repress a grin. She knew what had startled me.

"Your hair!"

She nodded.

"I mean, it looks great, but why? What happened?"

"Nothing happened, exactly. I just thought it was time to cut it. I got tired of accidentally sitting on the ends."

"Anything to do with the new project?"

She stood up to her full height, making me have to lift up my chin almost as high as it would go in order to keep her face in view. She tilted her head to the right, and a perfectly straight curtain of hair fell that direction.

"You know, I didn't think of that, but maybe. New production, new look."

"Have you submitted it?"

She nodded, bringing both her head and her hair back to their upright position.

"Good luck!"

"It's just a little local documentary film festival."

"Come on. It's a big deal and you know it. An award there could bring you some very useful attention, and probably more grants."

"I guess it could."

"Definitely."

"We'll find out soon if it will or not. How are you doing? What are you looking for today?"

"I'm consulting for the police again."

She opened her eyes wide and slowly turned up the corners of her mouth.

"Not for him."

Her mouth and eyelids drooped.

"Don't look so disappointed. He recommended me to another detective."

"Ah ha!"

"It doesn't mean anything personal. It's purely business."

"Mmhmm."

"Yes, all right, I'm seeing him on Saturday."

"I knew it!"

"Stop that."

"It's a big deal and you know it."

"I came to look up some records."

"Fine. Which forms do you need?"

As I was answering her question, she leaned through the door into the back room.

"Henry! Ella's here."

I got started filling out the appropriate forms, and soon Henry Park walked in, his crisp, wrinkleless button-down shirt tucked neatly into his flawlessly ironed pants.

"Henry, you always look perfect, and always exactly the same. How do you do that?"

"It's some kind of wizardry he does, a magic spell."

"Don't be ridiculous, Nadia. I'm just a boring man who likes to keep things simple."

Nadia and I both laughed. She went back to her piles of papers.

"Nonsense. You're fascinating and complicated and, according to Nadia, a wizard. How's the family?"

"Everyone's doing great, Ella. How are you?"

Before I could answer, Nadia looked up and smirked. "She's seeing that detective again."

"Do we have to discuss my personal life all the time?"

"Yours is the most interesting one."

"That can't be true. At least I hope it's not true, for your sakes."

I handed in the forms and was granted access to birth records and marriage records. I checked them all carefully. Every one confirmed the information I had been given. I still hadn't found anything remotely suspicious. No secrets. No lies.

I called Detective Figueroa from the car on the drive home, and told him everything was looking ordinary so far.

"I'll keep looking. That note on the victim must have meant something. I just haven't found it yet."

"That's what I figure. It wouldn't be a secret worth blackmailing about if it was easy to find. No one pays blackmail for something lots of people already know. Of course we don't actually have evidence of black-mail, of money, not yet anyway. Hey, would it help you to talk to the family? Do you think they could give you some leads?"

"It might. Do you think they would be willing to do that?"

"We can ask. It can't hurt. I'm going to the film set tomorrow to talk to Nina Chao again, and then I'm going to talk to the other sister, Olivia. I've talked to them both before, but I've got more questions now. Do you want to come with me?"

"Then they have already started filming?"

"Oh yeah, absolutely. They can't film at Olvera Street right now, since it's still a crime scene, but yeah, they are. I think they had to rearrange their schedule, but they're hard at work. Time is money, they say, in this case a lot of money."

"Okay. I'd appreciate a chance to ask a few questions. Thanks."

CHAPTER 5
Nina

The filming location that day was a park not far from my house in Santa Monica. Detective Figueroa stopped by and picked me up on his way there. Security on the set was pretty tight, but arriving with a police detective made it easy to get through. The detective and I were led directly to the area where the actors were housed in trailers while they waited for the next shot to be set up.

I saw Nina Chao standing in front of her trailer. She was instantly recognizable, partly because I had recently been watching videos of her old interviews, but perhaps more because she was one of those people who has what is called "the it factor". My logical brain would love to be able to pinpoint exactly what "it" is, but as far as I know, no one has ever been able to do that. That's why they call it "it". The person may not be the most beautiful one in the room, or the most talented, or the most intelligent, but the bulk of the attention gets focused on them anyway, because of whatever "it" is. Nina Chao was beautiful, and talented, and possibly also smart, but her most noticeable feature was "it".

She was talking to a much less noticeable young woman with thick, wavy, light brown hair. As the detective and I got closer, Nina's gaze shifted from her to us, and when the young woman noticed the change, she turned around, and I saw very pale skin and lots of freckles. The detective introduced me to Nina, and then she introduced the freckled girl to both of us as "my assistant Lucy".

The first thing Nina said to me was, "It's very pleasant to meet you." The slight variation on the usual phrase was deliberate, probably to make it memorable. She was not a person who was likely to miss an opportunity to make an impression. Her years of publicity training had sunk in, and were probably second nature to her now. There was undeniable ambition behind the clear eyes and the soft smile. Nina Chao had plans.

A tall woman in a plaid suit sped toward us on chunky heels, waving her phone in front of her as if she were trying to brush away mosquitoes.

"Excuse me! Who are you?"

Detective Figueroa flashed his badge. "Who are you?"

"Oh. Sorry Officer."

"It's Detective."

"Sorry. You can't be too careful, you know. There are crazy people out there."

Nina took a step toward the plaid woman.

"This is my agent, Carol Lychek."

"And I'm calling her lawyer." To prove she was serious, Ms. Lychek brought her phone down in front of her chest and started scrolling through it.

Nina touched her arm, slowing her scrolling. "It's all right, Carol. You don't have to do that."

"I think I do. You can't just go around talking to everybody about everything. Where's that girl, the studio publicist? Is she around here somewhere? Lucy, go find that girl."

"Actually, Lucy and I were just about to get some food. I don't think the publicist is here. Really, Carol.

It's fine. They only have a few questions, and it's important."

The agent's phone rang. She sighed.

"I have to take this."

Nina turned so that the agent was behind her and the detective and I were in front of her.

"Would you like to come with us? Craft service is just over here."

The four of us walked a few yards over to several tables laden with a wide variety of foods, everything from dressingless salads to glazed donuts, leaving Carol the agent yelling into her phone far behind us. Nina picked up a sandwich, and Lucy followed suit. Detective Figueroa and I abstained. We all sat at a picnic table.

"Ms. Chao, I know this is a difficult time for you, and a difficult subject to discuss, but have you been able to think of anyone who might have wanted to harm your sister?"

"Absolutely no one. I have been trying to think of someone, Detective, but I just can't come up with anything. Lucy can't either. We were discussing that earlier today."

"Really? Ms...., um, Lucy, what is your last name?"

"Moss."

"Ms. Moss. Did you know Hannah Chao well?"

"Well, I mean, we worked together. She was really helpful to me, especially when I first started the job."

"And when was that?"

"A few months ago."

"Really? So you knew her for a while."

"Yeah, I guess so. She was super nice. I really liked her."

"And you can't think of anyone who didn't like her?"

"No, no one. She got along with everybody."

Lucy's face suddenly started going all red underneath the freckles, and she kept glancing at something to my right, so I turned and looked in that direction.

A young man in tight clothes that displayed evidence of disciplined workouts and a highly restricted diet was walking toward our table. Nina noticed him too, and although she had more control over her reaction than Lucy did, her cheeks did get slightly pinker.

As the young man came closer, the scent of overapplied cologne announced the inevitability of his impending presence. He stopped next to Nina and flashed an expensive smile.

"I don't want to interrupt. I just thought I'd say a quick hello. Who are your guests?"

"This is Detective, um, sorry?"

"Figueroa."

"Detective Figueroa and Ms.?"

"Graepenteck."

"Mmhmm, and they're from the police."

The young man changed his expression abruptly to one of deep empathy.

"Oh, about your sister of course. It's so terrible. How are you holding up?"

"I'm doing all right."

"I'm really sorry. I shouldn't have interrupted."

"No, it's okay, really."

"I'll leave you alone. We can talk later."

He started to turn away, but Detective Figueroa stopped him with a question.

"Did you know Hannah Chao, Mr.?"

Lucy nearly dropped her sandwich on the ground, apparently horrified that the detective didn't know the young man's name. I didn't know it either, although he did look familiar. I had probably seen him in an ad somewhere, maybe on a billboard.

"I'm Anthony Kells." I had heard that name before. I had a vague recollection of a list. Was it one of those 30 under 30 things? Or perhaps he'd been nominated for something. He didn't seem insulted that the detective didn't know who he was, but he also didn't seem surprised by Lucy's reaction. He produced the exact same charming smile again. "Call me Tony."

"Did you know Hannah?"

"I wish I'd known her better. She was helping Nina out, and of course we've been working together on this film. I met her when we started rehearsals. We didn't talk much, unfortunately. She seemed like such a beautiful, dynamic person."

He glanced at Nina and she nodded appreciatively.

"So you two have been working together closely?"

"We have a lot of scenes together."

Tony and Nina both smiled. Lucy looked like she might have a panic attack.

"Ms. Chao, did your sister spend a lot of time on set with you?"

"Well we only started filming a little while ago, but yes, I liked having her with me. She helped me be less nervous."

"Are you nervous?"

"Very! Of course I am! This is a big role. It could be a big break for me. I'm very nervous about getting it right."

Tony wasn't going to miss that opportunity.

"She has no need to be nervous at all. She's brilliant, absolutely brilliant."

Nina looked down at the table as she smiled, and then looked up at Tony, striking the perfect balance of humility and appreciation. He smiled at her for a moment, and then turned back toward Detective Figueroa.

"If you don't have any more questions for me, I'll stop imposing on all of you."

Nina smiled wider. Lucy laughed as if Tony had just made a hilarious joke. Neither he nor Nina gave any indication that they'd heard her.

The detective nodded, and Tony walked away, bringing at least half the eyes in the surrounding area with him. Detective Figueroa got right back to business.

"I can understand that, being nervous, insecurity being part of the creative temperament and all. It can be a lot of pressure. I'm afraid I need to ask you again about the note we found in your sister's pocket, the one that said 'I know about your family'. Have you thought of anything that could possibly be referring to?"

"I'm sorry, Detective, but I have absolutely no idea. My parents raised us to be proud of every aspect of our heritage. We don't have any skeletons in our closet. At least, I don't know of any, but truly, I don't think there are any. My parents and my grandparents have always been very open and honest people. The only thing I can think of is that whoever gave that note to Hannah was mistaken. They must have gotten someone in our family confused with someone else."

"All right. Thank you. Ms. Graepenteck here is a genealogist. We've brought her into the investigation to try to find out what that note could have meant. Ms. Graepenteck, do you have any questions you would like to ask Ms. Chao?"

"I do, if you don't mind, Ms. Chao."

Her mouth was full of sandwich, but she nodded.

"Is there anyone, recently, here on the set or elsewhere, who asked questions about your family? Anyone who seemed particularly interested in it?"

Nina thought for a moment as she chewed. As she finished her mouthful, she shook her head.

"There really hasn't been anyone. Lucy, do you remember anyone asking about my family?"

Lucy shook her head. She was chewing too.

"Are there any stories about your family that you frequently tell? I was looking through some old interviews with you and your sisters, and you seem to have talked about your grandmother Rose Kahale Morales quite a bit. Are there other family members who come to mind often?"

"Our grandmother was a big influence on us. I guess all our grandparents have been, and our parents. Maybe I do talk about them from time to time. I can't think of specific stories I tell, though. I just mention them. I talk about the Chao family restaurants, how we grew up in them, worked in them. I talk about my grandmother and her family in Hawaii, I guess.

I do sometimes talk about how the Chao family and the Morales family have been in California for many generations. We are proud of our roots here. I don't think there's anything about any of it that would make someone write a note like that."

"Well, thank you. If you think of anything, let me or the detective know."

"I will."

We made sure that she had both my and Detective Figueroa's contact information, and started to leave, but the detective had one more thought.

"Ms. Chao, it does seem important that we found your sister on Olvera Street. I know you don't think anyone working on the film had a reason to harm her, but is there anyone else concerned with Olvera Street? Are there people who don't want you to film there, or who don't want the story of Olvera Street to be told? People who don't want this film made?"

"Not that I know of, but maybe that's a question for the director, or the producers."

Lucy quickly finished chewing a mouthful and bounced with enthusiasm.

"I think there is someone! A group, actually. I heard some people talking yesterday about some protesters. I didn't really catch it. I was just walking past and not really listening, but yes, I think there is some group that doesn't want this story told."

"Do you remember any details? What exactly they said? Who it was you heard talking?"

"No. I'm sorry. I wish I had paid more attention. I just didn't think. I didn't know the people, and I was just in a hurry to get to work. I wish I could be more help."

I heard a distant but nearing sound, reminiscent of the clop of an approaching horse, but overlaid with something like the squish of feet stepping in mud. I turned and saw plaid Carol charging toward us, sliding a little on her huge wedge heels. I nudged the detective. He took a quick look behind us and stood up.

"You've been very helpful, both of you. Thank you very much."

Detective Figueroa quickly scribbled down some notes, and we headed back to his car just as Carol reached shouting distance. She was yelling something as we walked away. I think I heard the word lawyer.

"So, Detective, do you think those protesters could be suspects?"

"It's possible. You never know. It's important to follow every lead. Was any of that helpful, about the family?"

"Not really. Maybe the other sister will be more informative."

"We'll see."

Chapter 6
Olivia

Olivia Chao, whose name was now Olivia Lawrence, lived in one of those pleasant but interchangeable neighborhoods in the San Fernando Valley. They were developed as middle class suburbs in the post-World War II building boom, and although they have been updated and well maintained, they tend to feel as if they haven't changed at all in the intervening decades. That was certainly true of this one. It was all small to medium-sized single family homes, punctuated by the occasional shopping center anchored by a grocery store. The streets were in an easy to navigate grid pattern, and the sidewalks were in good repair.

The house itself was lovely, an approximation of Craftsman style, but a thoughtfully created version, not like those appalling, out-of-proportion, boxy things that appear in more expensive neighborhoods.

The lawn was an arrangement of wildflowers contained by gravel pathways and rocky borders, standing out from its less imaginatively designed neighbors like the offering from the one truly talented student at a high school art show. We walked up to the small front porch, and Detective Figueroa rang the doorbell.

A tall man in khaki cargo pants and a striped golf shirt opened the door and offered his hand to me and then to Detective Figueroa for shaking.

"I'm Jake Lawrence. Hello, Detective. My wife is this way."

We followed him into an airy living room, bright with sunlight. It was decorated in bland neutrals, with a light grey carpet and a navy blue sofa and matching armchairs. It was hard to reconcile the flair of the exterior with the dullness of the interior. Perhaps they thought that, because of all that light, the room didn't need any additional color. I looked around a bit more and quickly formed a new theory. The many photos in the room provided evidence that Olivia and Jake had four small children. It had to be a case of prioritizing easy maintenance over aesthetics. The room did look surprisingly clean for a house with that many kids in it.

At the back of the room was an archway leading to what must have been the kitchen. I could see beige linoleum and an open back door. At least two children were playing in the yard. Jake Lawrence lifted up a toddler who was grasping one of the sofa cushions and walked through the archway and straight through the back door, closing it behind him and nodding to someone in the kitchen on his way out.

A lean woman in jeans, a chambray button-down, and bare feet came out of the kitchen, smiling and extending her hand. Her most striking feature was her perfectly straight, exactly even, chin length bob, just as tidy and glossy as Nadia's, but significantly shorter and with thick bangs. It was right out of a silent film, although Olivia did not have the overplucked eyebrows and heavy lipstick to match.

"Hello, Detective. How can I help you?"

"This is Ms. Graepenteck, a consultant with the department. We have just a few questions for you."

She invited us to sit on the sofa, and established before we sat down that we weren't in need of anything to eat or drink. Olivia sat in one of the armchairs with crossed ankles and remarkably erect posture. In her blue clothes on the blue chair, she looked as if she were about to be photographed for a magazine cover. She closed her eyes and sighed as she accepted my condolences about her sister, and her face remained relaxed as she told the detective that she still had no idea who could possibly have had any desire to kill Hannah.

She maintained her calm demeanor as I asked about her extended family. In fact, when I mentioned Rose Kahale she relaxed even more, and leaned forward as she spoke.

"Our grandmother Rose, we called her Tutu, was such an important force in our family. It's been several years now since she passed away, and we all still miss her very much. She was our family's heart, so full of love and warmth and unconditional support. We were lucky to have her as long as we did."

Any publicist would have been proud of that speech, and the gentle smile that followed it, but after taking a breath she added a sentence that sounded much less rehearsed. I started to think she might ease her way into letting her guard down.

"Just thinking about her still makes me happy."

"I can see that it does. I noticed that, when you and your sisters gave interviews for Brite, you mentioned your grandmother often."

"Did we? Probably. As I said, she was a very important part of our lives."

"Did people often ask you about your family?"

"Not that much. We were told to talk about how multicultural we are, so we did that, but people were usually more interested in what we were wearing and how we wore our hair and if we were dating anyone."

"Has anybody shown an interest in your family more recently?"

"What do you mean? I don't give interviews anymore, not that I get many requests for them. I'm not in that world now."

"Nobody has tried to contact you, to ask questions about your family?"

Olivia's shoulders began to tighten, and the openness engendered by discussion of her grandmother faded away. "No. Why would they?"

"So, you aren't interested in the entertainment industry anymore?"

She shook her head slowly. "Not. At. All. I had enough of that as a teenager."

"But your sister Nina is."

The tension in her shoulders increased. "Nina is different."

"How so?"

Her gaze had been drifting around the room, but now her eyes were directly on me. The look in them showed no antagonism yet, but it was veering dangerously close to being a glare. "We've just always had very different personalities. She's always been more interested in being the center of attention. That never mattered so much to me."

The tension in her shoulders had traveled up her neck and was now reaching her mouth. She clearly was not enjoying discussing this topic, which could have been merely a reflection of ordinary sibling rivalry, or it could have been something more unusual, and more specific.

"This film role must be important for her, and your sister Hannah must have thought so too. Wasn't she working with Nina, helping her with her career?"

The tension worked its way all the way up to Olivia's eyes. Now she was definitely glaring at me, although there was also a shininess that hadn't been there before. Was she about to cry?

She turned her head toward the kitchen. "I probably should go check on the kids. It sounds like they're fighting out there."

The detective and I assured her that we didn't hear anything, but that had no effect on her.

"I need to go check on the kids."

She stood up abruptly and rushed through the kitchen and out the back door.

I turned to Detective Figueroa. "Isn't her husband out there with the kids?"

"Yeah, that was strange. She's definitely upset. I don't know why. There wasn't much reason. You were just getting started, and neither one of us mentioned blackmail yet, or the note."

"That's right."

We sat there on the sofa, waiting for Olivia to return. To pass the time, I looked around the bright yet bland room. The family photos took up almost every available space, hanging on the walls and cluttering up the surfaces.

"Have you looked at all these photos?"

"There are a lot of them. They're everywhere."

"Yes, but it's not just that. They're mostly of Olivia, Jake, and their kids, which I suppose is normal, but then there are quite a few with those people, that older couple. I'm guessing they're Jake's parents. I don't see the Chao family though."

"Huh. You're right. There aren't any of them." He moved his head around slowly, studying all the walls and shelves and tabletops. "Well there is that one."

The detective pointed at one photo on the wall, near the back of the living room, near a window, almost hidden by a curtain. It was indeed a photo of the Chao family, when the girls were teenagers. They weren't dressed up in popstar costumes, but they were stiffly and unnaturally arranged, as if for a Christmas card photo.

"Oh yes. Is that the only one?"

"I think so. I don't see any others."

We both turned toward the kitchen, because we heard the sound of footsteps. They were too loud to be barefoot.

That was because it was not Olivia, but Jake, who emerged. He headed straight for us and almost aggressively ushered us out the front door.

"I'm sorry, but I think that's all my wife can handle for today. She's still very upset about her sister, and talking about it is very difficult for her. You're going to have to come back another time."

We didn't resist, and got back in the car.

"Detective, I don't know about you, but I got the sense there was something going on there other than grief."

"I got the exact same sense, that same feeling. There's something about Olivia's relationship with her family that she doesn't want to talk about."

CHAPTER 7
The Bicycle

It was Friday, so I drove up the winding Laurel Canyon side roads to my mother's house, the house my great grandfather Patrick de Brisay III built, for dinner. I was once again grateful for my tiny car as I stayed smack in the middle of the narrow, shoulderless roads, the view to one side being nothing but vegetation, due to the steep incline upward, and the view to the other side being nothing but sky, due to the abrupt cliff edge, hoping not to have to contend with anyone coming the other direction. There had been an unusual amount of rain in recent weeks, and no fires yet, so everything on the vegetation side was pleasantly green, which somehow made the precarious drive feel a bit less intimidating. Finally, I turned up Alta Brea Crescent and went all the way to the top of the hill. I punched in the code to open the tall iron gate, drove under the giant palm fronds and around the circular driveway, and parked in front of the steps up to the wide stone terrace.

My mother was already standing in the doorway, waving at me. Usually she just waited for me inside.

"Is something wrong?"

"No, not at all. It's just that your timing is perfect! I'm trying a new salmon recipe, and I just took it out of the oven. We really should taste it within the next few minutes if we want to judge it properly."

"All right then."

I followed her down the corridor to the kitchen. She lit the candles and we rushed through our somewhat modified versions of the shabbat blessings, and then she served up the salmon, along with some asparagus and little red potatoes.

"It's delicious, Mom, but since when are you so concerned with recipes?"

"It's a new interest. I read some articles and got inspired."

"Fair enough."

In addition to more details about her new interest in cooking, she told me about some articles she had read about discoveries concerning black holes, and a study of the interaction between a certain species of fish and the coral reefs it inhabited. I told her about the discovery of Hannah Chao's body and my new project with Detective Figueroa. Soon the dinner was done and cleared and we were finishing our ice cream, our spoons clanging against our bowls as we scooped up the rapidly melting remnants.

"What's bothering you, Ella? Something other than this police case is on your mind."

"There is something, actually, a small thing."

"Yes?"

"You know that little golden bicycle, with the wheels that turn, the one Grandfather Graepenteck gave me just before he died?"

"Sure, the one his father brought over from Germany."

"That's the one. I can't find it."

"What do you mean? You lost it?"

"I can't have lost it. I never take it anywhere. It has to be in the house. It's never anyplace else."

"But you can't find it."

"It's not on the shelf where it belongs, and it doesn't seem to be any other place either."

"Could someone have taken it?"

"No. No one's been in the house lately, and I know I saw it a week or so ago, and I can't imagine anyone would break in and just take that and nothing else."

"Strange."

"It has to be somewhere in the house. Either it fell and got knocked behind or underneath something, or I somehow don't remember moving it."

"You'll find it."

"I'm sure I will."

"Are you seeing that other detective again soon?"

"You mean Detective Roth? I'm seeing him tomorrow, actually."

"Ah."

"What?"

"Nothing."

"What do you mean by 'ah'?"

"I just think it's interesting that you lost your grandfather's bicycle just as things are getting more serious with this man."

"I wouldn't say they're getting serious, and even if they are, the two things have nothing to do with each other."

"Okay."

"What do you mean by 'okay'?"

"You know I'm no aficionado of Freud, but sometimes coincidences aren't coincidences."

"And sometimes a bicycle is just a bicycle, and yes I know the cigar thing is apocryphal, and of course this bicycle isn't just a bicycle."

"No. It's a symbol of your close relationship with your grandfather, that he gave you just before he left you."

"He didn't leave me. He died."

"Dying is a kind of leaving."

"It's not the same at all, and I know you have this theory about me and this supposed fear of intimacy, but this is one of those admittedly rare instances in which you are just plain wrong."

"I didn't say anything about your fear of intimacy. I think it's interesting that you would bring that up."

"Mom!"

"All right, all right."

"Meanwhile, I do have this case I need to work on. I'm not getting anywhere interesting on that either.

The Chao family must have some kind of secret, but so far I just can't find anything."

"I'm sure you'll dig it up."

"There's almost always something about their family people don't want to talk about. This family seems to be proud of every aspect of their history, but there just has to be something."

I gave up on getting any more ice cream out of my bowl and stood up and brought it to the sink. While I was rinsing it out, my back to my mother, I said, "Sometimes when I'm doing research, especially if I'm looking for secrets, I start thinking about our family."

"The Graepentecks don't have any secrets."

"Not the Graepentecks."

"Oh."

"I know the de Brisays aren't your favorite topic, but there are a lot of interesting stories there."

"I suppose interesting is one word for them."

"Sometimes I think about your grandfather, and how his brothers got involved in, you know, shady enterprises, but he didn't. I wonder about that."

"I don't know that he was so much more moral than they were. He was the eldest, and he felt a certain responsibility. He wanted to uphold the family name or some such. That's what he told me, anyway."

"You asked him about that?"

"We were close. I was his only grandchild."

"I wish I could have known him."

"My dad was a lot like him."

"I'm glad I got to know him."

"I'm glad too. I know you weren't as close to him as you were to your Grandfather Graepenteck, but I'm glad he was in your life."

I finished rinsing out my ice cream bowl, and then I turned back toward the table and saw that my mother was finished with hers, so I picked that up and rinsed it too. When I turned back around again I saw that she was staring at me, with an oddly squinty look around her eyes.

"Why have you been thinking about the de Brisays? Something came up, didn't it? In this investigation you're doing, this police thing, something came up."

"Only tangentially. I saw one name, but it probably has nothing to do with..."

"What name?"

"It's not even..."

"What name?"

"Nicholas de Brisay III."

I was surprised to see her shoulders actually relax. She suggested we bring some tea into the living room and discuss the situation further. I didn't see much point, but I agreed.

We sat in two of the faded green velvet armchairs by the enormous fireplace, and I provided more details about the film, the case, the relationship between them. She nodded the whole time. When I'd finished, she took a long sip of tea, and then a deep breath, and then she surprised me again.

"Nicholas isn't so bad."

"Really?"

"I mean he's as sleazy as can be, and I would never do business with him, or trust him, in any way, with anything, but he's not as bad as some of them."

"I vaguely recall meeting him, I think."

"Once or twice, when you were small."

She was staring into her tea. She took another sip, without looking up. I didn't want to interrupt her concentration, so I just sat and waited. Finally she spoke.

"I don't think you need to worry about him. Just ignore it."

It was probably good advice.

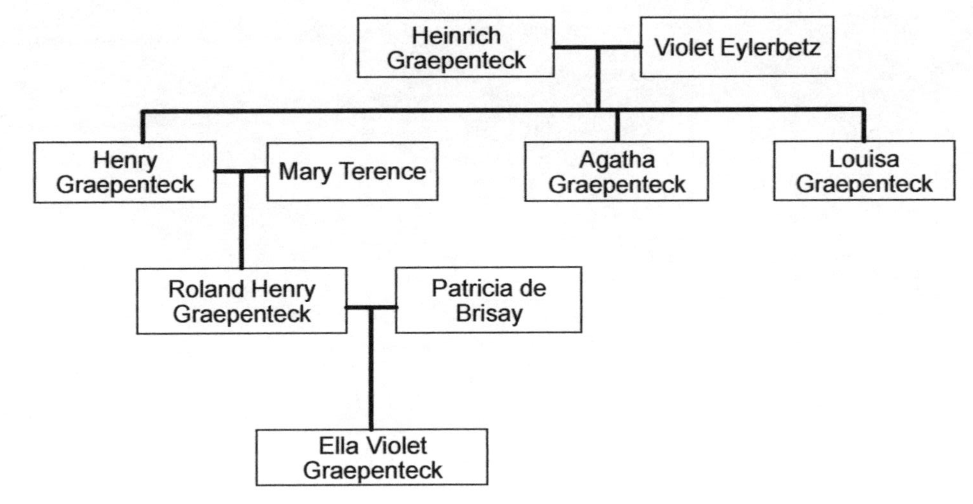

Heinrich Graepenteck
Violet Eylerbetz
Henry Graepenteck
Mary Terence
Agatha Graepenteck
Louisa Graepenteck
Roland Henry Graepenteck
Patricia de Brisay
Ella Violet Graepenteck

CHAPTER 8

The Parents

Unfortunately, I have a bad habit of not taking good advice.

It occurred to me that Nicholas de Brisay III would know a lot about the film, and maybe something about the protesters Lucy Moss had mentioned, and therefore it was possible that he would know something about the murder. He would probably be a good person to question. I thought I should seriously consider suggesting that to Detective Figueroa.

I had gotten to the point of searching for contact info for de Brisay when my phone rang. It was, of all people, Detective Figueroa. I might almost have considered it a sign from the Universe, if I believed in those things.

"I'm going to Encino to ask some questions. I need to talk to the parents of the victim, so I'm about to drive over there, to their house. Do you want to come with me?"

"To Edward and Christina Chao's house?"

"Yeah, I've got a couple of things to ask them."

"I do, yes."

That seemed like an opportunity I shouldn't miss. I didn't want to complicate things with a discussion about my second cousin once removed, especially about the possibility of his creating a conflict of interest situation for me, so the idea of making contact with him was pushed to the side. Maybe I would take my mother's advice after all, and forget all about Nicholas de Brisay III.

Detective Figueroa talked almost the entire ride to Encino, reviewing every detail of the case. It seemed to be his way of mulling things over in his mind. I prefer quieter ways, but when you're working with other people, you need to be accepting of different modes of operation. I didn't want to interfere with his process, so I allowed my mind to wander, although I made sure to nod and make acknowledging noises from time to time.

I thought about the case too, part of the time. I also thought, a lot of the time, about where the little gold bicycle my grandfather gave me could be. I tried to come up with something new, some place I hadn't yet looked, but I had no success. The rest of the time, assorted unimportant thoughts appeared, completely out of nowhere, such as what Detective Cormac Roth might be doing at that moment, absolutely random non sequiturs like that. The human mind is unpredictable.

Finally we arrived at the house, large but ordinary, white with blue shutters and a tidy lawn. Mr. Chao opened the door before we reached it, and then ushered us in.

Every surface in the Chao home was cluttered with trinkets. There were framed photos everywhere, and small statues of animals, especially horses and dogs. There were souvenir plates and glasses, piles of books of varying sizes, and assorted other knickknacks. Brightly colored textiles from different countries hung on the walls. It was an overwhelming assault on the eyes, but once I had a chance to acclimate

I noticed that there was not a speck of dust anywhere. It was cluttered, but it was clean.

Edward Chao was well over six feet tall, clearly the source of all three of his daughters' height, as his wife Christina did not quite reach five feet. He guided the detective and me to some creaky but sturdy chairs, and she brought us each a cup of tea, without asking whether or not either of us wanted one. He sat across a coffee table covered in books and photos from us, in a matching chair, and she stood in the doorway to the kitchen, occasionally disappearing into it, and frequently dabbing her eyes with a bright blue hand-kerchief.

Once we were all settled, the detective started his questions.

"I'm sorry to impose on you at such a difficult time. We will be as brief as possible. We just need confirmation of some facts."

Mr. Chao nodded.

"Are you aware of any group that is trying to stop the Sterling film from being made? Any people planning a protest, or wanting to keep them from shooting at Olvera Street?"

"I never heard about anything like that."

"Are you sure your daughter Hannah never gave any indication of a threat against her, or against her sister Nina, or against the film? She didn't say anything un-usual, or behave strangely, seem upset?"

"Not that I remember. Everything seemed normal."

Over in the kitchen doorway, Christina Chao's blue handkerchief was put to work again.

"Is there anything you have thought of since the last time we talked? Anything that came to mind? Anything you think I should know?"

"No. Nothing at all."

Detective Figueroa indicated with raised eyebrows and a quick nod that it was my turn to ask questions.

I unfolded a printout of the family tree I had con-structed, moved some books to make room to spread it out on the coffee table, and asked for confirmation of the information it contained. This enticed Mrs. Chao out from the doorway and fully into the room. The two of them perused the diagram, and Mr. Chao declared it correct. His wife still didn't seem ready to talk, so I avoided directing any questions to her. I didn't want to scare her back into the kitchen.

"I get the impression that you and your daughters discuss your extended family often."

"Yes, family is very important to us. We talk about it all the time."

"Are there family stories that have been passed down, that you have shared with your daughters?"

"Oh yes, and more than that. We have photographs." Edward nodded to Christina, and she walked over to a shelf and pulled down a large photo album. That shelf and several more were packed with more albums. I moved the family tree so she had room to open the book on the table, and for the next hour or so Detective Figueroa and I were presented with photo after photo and regaled with recitations of tales that Mr. Chao must have told hundreds of times before. Once or twice, in the middle of a story, Mrs. Chao very nearly smiled.

My favorite of all those photos was one from their wedding, with the two of them between their respective parents. On the far left was Robert Chao, whose face reflected his many generations of Chinese ancestry, and next to him, and several inches taller, his blonde wife June, who looked like a Victorian illustration of a Viking maiden. Then there was Edward, even taller than his mother, and next to him tiny Christina. Neither of her parents was much taller than she was, giving an overall effect of the highest peaks of the Rocky Mountains right next to the Great Plains. David Morales' dark skin and June Wallace Chao's pale skin made each other stand out more starkly, and Christina's mother Rose, adorned with an array of fresh flowers, looked like an ad luring tourists to Hawaii. This dramatically eclectic group resulted in the ethnically indeterminate beauty that allowed fans of so many different backgrounds to identify with the Chao sisters. It was the whole DNA story in one snapshot.

They had many old photos, going all the way back to the 1880s, but almost all were of the Chinese ancestors and the Hawaiian ones. Those were the ones they wanted to talk about. They didn't seem very interested in his mother's family or her father's. I found that curious, but I didn't want to cause them extra stress, and I was afraid if I pressed them at all I would lose any chance of getting more useful information. I was trying to formulate a question that would lead them in the right direction without making them shut down completely when Detective Figueroa interjected.

He picked up the family tree I had left on the floor between us, spread it out on top of the photos we were all looking at, and started pointing.

"You have told us a lot of interesting things about these ancestors and these ancestors, but we haven't heard much about these or these. I'm sure you have interesting stories about them too. Can you tell us some of those?"

Any trace of a smile disappeared from Christina's face, and the blue handkerchief, which had been retired to a pocket, emerged again. At least she didn't run off to the kitchen. Edward started closing photo albums.

"I think that's about all we can manage today, Detective. I'm sorry, but this is still very difficult for us."

I was feeling some anger at Detective Figueroa as we walked back to his car. I was weighing whether or not to tell him that I thought we could have gleaned more information if he had been more sensitive. I decided that once we were in the car with the doors closed I would say something, but he spoke before I had the chance.

"You probably think that was insensitive of me, that it wasn't a good question, but I don't think they were going to tell us anything else. I wanted to make sure they were avoiding his mother's family and her father's family on purpose, and not by accident. That question made it clear."

I had to consider the possibility that his point of view might have some merit. I wasn't fully convinced, but somehow the fact that he had done it on purpose, as a strategy, rather than blundering into it, made my anger subside. A reasonable disagreement about tactics didn't bother me so much. The situation did make me realize, however, that I had never had that kind of difficulty when I was working with Detective Roth. Our methods always blended together much more easily. It wasn't a time to be thinking about him though. Detective Figueroa was waiting for some response from me.

"Well, we know now that there are some issues in this family, with Olivia, and with these two ancestral branches. At least we've moved from nothing at all, to maybe something."

The detective nodded his head. "Right. That's what I think. We're making progress. We have possible leads."

As we drove away, I felt an odd internal pang. Was I actually missing Cormac Roth? The thought of calling him as soon as I got home entered my mind, but I pushed it away immediately. It was a ridiculous idea. I would be having dinner with him that night. Anything I might want to say to him could certainly wait a few hours.

CHAPTER 9

New Hampshire

Detective Figueroa drove me back to the sanctuary of my peaceful little house, which is painted a pale yellow called Sunwash that makes it look like the sun is always shining on it. There, I continued mulling everything the various Chaos had said. They had all claimed to be bewildered by the idea that there could be any sort of family secret they would want to hide. Yet, the Chao parents were curiously uninterested in discussing his mother's family or her father's, while they were delighted to share as many details as possible about the other branches of the family. Also, middle sister Olivia had become surprisingly upset at the mention of Nina's film role and Hannah's involvement in it. Maybe the family secret was a more recent one, not about the ancestors at all.

It was the ancestors who were my area of expertise, though, so that was where I needed to put my focus.

It would be a good use of my time to look for more information about them. I decided to start with Mr. Chao's mother, and see if there was anything interesting to find in her family.

Edward Chao's birth certificate listed his mother's maiden name as June Wallace, and her birthplace as New Hampshire. I had seen that before, but I doublechecked to confirm. Her marriage certificate to Robert Chao, in 1957, listed her name as June Wallace, her birthplace as New Hampshire, and her year of birth as 1938. All was consistent so far. It also listed her parents' names as Harold and Emily Wallace.

I had been unable to find a birth certificate for her. If she had been born in 1938, however, there were all kinds of reasons why one might not exist. It might never have existed. Back then not everyone had a birth certificate, and its being in the midst of the Great Depression would make it even more likely that some documentation just never got done, especially if there was any sort of fee involved in getting it done. Even if there had at some point been a birth certificate, there are many ways it could have been accidentally destroyed. I wasn't going to devote a whole lot of time to trying to find a document that likely didn't exist.

What I would try to do is to find her on the 1940 US federal census. Usually the first thing I do when I'm trying to find out about a person's life is find them on a census. It's a snapshot in time that often yields useful clues.

There was no listing in the census index for a June Wallace of the right age, so I looked for her parents. There were many listings for a Harold Wallace, eleven of them in New Hampshire. I clicked through and viewed the page for each of those eleven, and only one had a wife named Emily. They lived in a small town called Wingfield. Just the two of them were listed in the house, though. There were no children.

It was possible that was the correct family, and June was just left off the list by mistake. I have come across that situation more than once before. I decided to look for other couples named Harold and Emily Wallace, though, in case they had moved from New Hampshire already by that time.

I spent quite a while eliminating Harold and Emily Wallaces and Wallises and Walls and Walts, including

Harrys and Emmas and Amelias, and became more and more convinced that the couple I had found in Wingfield, New Hampshire was the right couple. I decided to look for more information about them.

I looked for a Harold Wallace in Wingfield on the 1930 census, and found just one. He was the right age, and so probably the same man. I looked through New Hampshire marriage records to see if I could find him there, but I didn't. Marriage records can be missing for the same kinds of reasons that birth records can, so I thought I'd see if I could find Emily anyway.

I took a chance that Emily was also from Wingfield, which was a very small town, so I searched for every Emily there of near the right age on the 1930 census. There was only one. Her name was Emily Longwell, and she lived with her parents and six siblings.

I found both the Wallace and Longwell families on the 1920 census as well, which provided no new information, and then I moved forward in time and started looking for all the family members in 1940.

I did the Wallaces first, as they were a smaller family. Harold had just one brother, Louis, who was married with two children in 1940, and had his widowed mother living with him. That was the whole rest of the family.

The Longwells took a bit longer. The parents were both still alive in 1940, living with the youngest children. Most of the older children were married and living with their spouses, some with children. There was no other Emily of the right age in Wingfield. When I got to Emily's brother Horace and his family, I stopped and reread every line very carefully.

Horace and his wife had just one child, a two year old daughter, named June.

This was certainly not anything close to decisive proof, but it was some very suggestive circumstantial evidence. If Emily Longwell was Emily Wallace, and Horace Longwell was her brother, and June Longwell was his daughter, then June Wallace Chao was really June Longwell Chao, and Emily Wallace was her aunt, not her mother.

If this was a family secret, it wasn't a very juicy one. There were lots of reasons a child might be raised by a relative such as an aunt, few of them things that the family would feel a need to hide. Nevertheless, it was the first thing I had found in this family that was at all out of the ordinary, and it felt like a significant find. I felt like a success.

out of the ordinary, and it felt like a success.

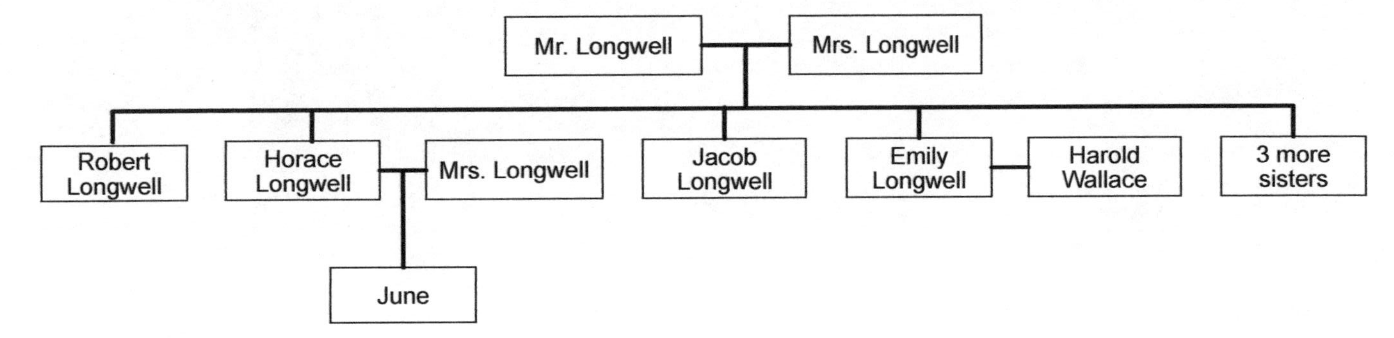

Mr. Longwell
Mrs. Longwell
Robert Longwell
Horace Longwell
Mrs. Longwell
June
Jacob Longwell
Emily Longwell
Harold Wallace
3 more sisters

CHAPTER 10

The Longwells

It was Saturday night, and I was having dinner with Cormac Roth. We were at a comfortable, homey, Italian restaurant. I had a very tasty eggplant parmigiana, and he was enjoying a thick slice of lasagna. He was telling me about the case he had just solved. It had nothing to do with genealogy, but I was enjoying hearing about it nonetheless.

"You and Detective Vasquez really are an excellent team."

"We do clear a lot of cases. This one wasn't complicated though."

"I'm sure you're just being modest."

"No. It wasn't a tough one, and why are you still calling him Detective Vasquez?"

"Oh, I don't know. It's just..."

"What did he say he wants you to call him?"

"I know. He wants me to use his first name. It's just taking me some time to get used to that."

"Well, sort of. Nobody calls him Rafael. None of his friends, anyway. What did he say?"

Cormac's tone was warm, but gently mocking. His smile matched it.

I sighed.

He just kept smiling.

"He wants me to call him Raf."

"Yes! And I'm?"

"Mac."

"Hey! There you go!"

"I'm not really that stuffy, am I?"

"Not stuffy, just formal, businesslike."

"Well, we met doing formal business. I guess I'm just having a little trouble transitioning."

"You're doing fine, and it's kind of cute."

"Cute? Really?"

"I said kind of cute, for the time being, anyway."

"Okay, Mac."

"Bravo!"

"Thank you."

"So, speaking of formal business, how's your investigation going?"

"Well, actually, I finally found something interesting."

"Good! Last time we talked, it sounded like you were finding it pretty boring."

"Not so much boring as frustrating. For a long time, the Chao family seemed to be completely devoid of secrets, but I finally turned up something, maybe."

"And what's that, Ella?" As he said my name he looked at me expectantly. I took the hint.

"Well, Mac,"

He smiled and nodded.

"I don't really have conclusive evidence, but it looks like Edward Chao's mother was raised by people who weren't her biological parents."

"And that was a secret?"

"It seems so. It's not a very serious secret though. I don't think it's something worth paying blackmail over."

"So she was adopted?"

"I don't know if she was legally adopted. It looks like she was raised by her aunt. She went by June Wallace, until she married Robert Chao, but it looks like her biological parents were Mrs. Wallace's brother and his wife. Her birth name was June Longwell."

"Longwell? Like the Longwell brothers?"

"Who?"

"You never heard of them? They were famous bank robbers, back in the 1930s, into the 1940s."

"Really?"

"They robbed 52 banks, all over the east coast."

"52?"

"The joke was one for every week of the year, but of course it was more than one year, and they didn't do it every week. It was about ten years, I think. They finally got caught, but most of the money was never recovered."

"Did they spend it all?"

"They couldn't have. They hid it somewhere. Every once in a while someone tries to find it, but no one ever does. It probably got destroyed somehow, burned in a house fire, or lost at sea. It could be buried some-place, but people have dug up every likely spot."

"Were they from New Hampshire?"

"Maybe. New England, definitely."

"Was Horace Longwell one of the bank robbing brothers?"

"Robert, Horace, and Jacob. Horace was the middle brother."

"Yes, that's right, that's this family, and there were four sisters. One of them was Emily, and she became Mrs. Wallace."

"Maybe you've found a juicier secret than you thought."

"Bank robbing brothers."

"The family business."

"Maybe I really have found something."

"Congratulations."

"Thanks. I'm looking forward to having something to tell Detective Figueroa."

"How's that going, by the way, working with him?"

"Fine. Good. He's smart."

"Yeah, he is."

"He does..."

"What?"

"I'm sorry. I know he's your friend, and it's really nothing."

"What?"

"Well, he does, talk kind of a lot."

Cormac laughed. "That's not really your style, is it?"

"It's not a big deal. It's fine. He's smart. He's a good detective."

"Yeah."

"It's not like working with you though."

He smiled wide and stared at me. "We work well together, don't we?"

"We do." I could feel my face turning red. They had probably turned the heat up in the restaurant. "So, do you know a lot about the history of bank robbing? Is that a hobby of yours?"

"I can tell you some good bank robber stories."

"That sounds fun. Yes, please."

CHAPTER 11

The Aunts

Aunt Louisa, my grandfather Graepenteck's sister, was away on one of her frequent explorations of the wide world of five star hotels, and Aunt Agatha, also my grandfather's sister, and her husband were staying in her house in Pasadena while she was gone. Aunt Agatha loves an opportunity to housesit. Unlike her sister, she much prefers the comforts of home to the lap of luxury, although when Aunt Louisa's house is the home, there isn't much difference.

I hadn't been to see Aunt Agatha since she had arrived in town, and she would be leaving in a few days, so before I met up with Detective Figueroa I went over there to spend some time with her. We were sitting in the room at the top of the main staircase that Aunt Louisa likes to call, appropriately enough, the sitting room.

"I'm telling you, Aunt Agatha, it probably wasn't dangerous at all, but it scared me half to death. It's been nearly a month now, and I still get nervous every time I reach that patch of sidewalk. I was just walking along, and all of a sudden, out of nowhere, this snake appeared. I don't know what kind it was, but it wasn't a rattler. It had long black and yellow stripes."

"It was close enough for you to see it clearly, then?"

"Yes, very clearly! It moved so quickly, just whipped right across my path and disappeared into the brush, but those markings were memorable."

"That was a striped racer."

Aunt Agatha hadn't even looked up from her crossword puzzle to make that pronouncement.

"There's a snake actually called a striped racer?"

"Oh yes. There are lots of them around here. They're one of the most common species in California."

"It was the first time I'd seen one."

She laughed. "Well, they don't make a point of being seen."

"And I don't exactly seek them out. I must admit, it's a perfect name. That snake's two most obvious qualities were its stripes and its speed."

"It's an excellent name. I wish everything were named so well."

"They aren't dangerous, I assume, striped racers?"

"Oh no, nothing to worry about, not for humans."

"Good. Thanks. That's a relief."

She nodded, but still never looked up.

There were sounds outside the room. I thought I heard the front door closing, and then footsteps on the stairs, but Aunt Agatha gave no indication of having heard anything. I was just about to ask her if she expected anyone when Aunt Louisa appeared in the doorway to the corridor, arms outstretched to allow the wide sleeves of her lavender blouse to array themselves like butterfly wings.

"Hello everyone! I'm home!"

At that, Aunt Agatha looked up briefly, smiled, said, "Hello, Dear. I thought you weren't coming until tomorrow," and went right back to her crossword puzzle.

"Change of plans. It's so nice to see you, Ella Darling. How are you?"

"I'm well, thank you. How was your trip?"

"Delightful, but that's a tale for another time. I'm so glad you're here! It's such a nice surprise in any case, but especially now, because I have something to show you. I was going to have it wrapped, but I'd rather not wait. When an opportunity presents itself, one must embrace it! Would you be a dear and go bring up my small case from downstairs? I left it by the door. Ana won't be back until tomorrow, and you are so much stronger and more youthful than I."

When I returned with her carry on bag, she was draped across a chair, leaning over Aunt Agatha, apparently offering suggestions for answers to crossword clues. She stood up as soon as she saw me, waving her sleeves in my direction.

"Ah, yes, there it is. Put it up here on the table."

She opened the bag, plunged her hand deep into the middle of it, and pulled out a small box. She handed it to me.

"Look inside."

As I did so, I couldn't restrain myself from gasping.

"It's just like the bicycle Grandfather gave me!"

"It is, isn't it?"

"But it's a carriage. I love it! The wheels spin and everything. Where did you get it?"

"I finally got around to seeing the village the Graepentecks came from."

"Gardewald?"

"That's the one. I kept meaning to go there, but somehow I just never did. There's not much to it, just some houses and a couple of shops, but in one of the shops I saw this, and I thought of you, Darling, and my dear late brother, and Papa, and, well, it was all quite emotional really, and I just had to buy it for you. You know your father was the closest thing I had to a son, which makes you the closest thing I have to a granddaughter."

"I know, Aunt Louisa. It's wonderful. Thank you so much!"

"You're most welcome."

I gave her a kiss on the cheek, but then I had to confess.

"You know, the timing of this is very interesting, because, well, unfortunately, at the moment, I am unable to find Grandfather's little bicycle."

"What do you mean?"

"I mean I can't find it. It's gone missing, somehow, from the shelf where it belongs."

"Did someone take it?"

"I don't see how anyone could have."

"Well then where has it gone?"

"I don't know."

Aunt Agatha not only looked up, but actually put aside her crossword puzzle.

"You've lost Papa's bicycle?"

"It's not lost, Aunt Agatha. It's just temporarily missing."

She squinted her eyes and tilted her head. "Euphemizing won't change the situation."

"I'll find it. I promise you both, it's somewhere in my house, and I will find it."

Aunt Louisa took a step toward me and stage whispered, "Maybe you should ask that handsome detective to look for it."

Aunt Agatha let out a high-pitched laugh. I would almost call it a squeal. "Oh yes! How is your detective?"

"He's not my detective."

"Aggie, look how she's blushing."

"I see it. Her cheeks are bright pink!"

"I'm just agitated about Grandfather's bicycle."

"Don't try to change the subject. What is happening between you and the handsome, charming detective?"

I could see there was no way to escape. I capitulated. "We're, I mean, I suppose you could say we're seeing each other."

Aunt Agatha semi-squealed again. Aunt Louisa arranged herself on a small couch upholstered in peach silk, which complemented her lavender blouse, and patted the empty space beside her. "Come sit with me here, on the loveseat."

"Very subtle."

"That is what this piece of furniture is called."

I sat. Both aunts stared at me.

"There's really nothing to tell."

They continued to stare.

"We had dinner together Saturday night."

Aunt Agatha actually clapped her hands.

"He helped me with some research I'm doing."

"Oh, Darling, you didn't discuss work!"

"We both enjoy our work."

"Ella, this is why Aggie and I worry about you."

Aunt Agatha nodded.

"I'm perfectly fine."

"We worry that you might have the smallest tendency to keep people at a distance, just the teensiest little bit of a fear of…"

"Oh God. Not you too. I'm not afraid of intimacy."

Both aunts looked at me sympathetically.

"I'm not!"

CHAPTER 12
Central Division

For the first time, I actually went to see Detective Figueroa at his police station downtown. It was on my way home from Pasadena. It looked very different from the Hollywood police station, although both were made primarily of brick. This one had an enormous mural painted all the way across the front of it, and a couple of tall, leafy trees growing out of the sidewalk, on either side of the mural. Their shade provided some small relief from the afternoon heat.

Inside, it was a warren of corridors lined with grey doors. A uniformed officer led me to the correct one, and it opened onto a room that had no windows but felt bright and spacious. I looked up and realized that was because it had a high ceiling dotted with skylights. The skylights seemed not to have been cleaned in a while, but the light came through nevertheless. The detective walked over to greet me and invited me to sit in a black plastic chair in front of his grey metal desk.

"So, Ms. Graepenteck, you had something you wanted to tell me about, something you wanted to discuss?"

"Does the name Longwell mean anything to you?"

He was silent for several seconds, leaning back in his chair and bouncing a few times. It was something I had seen Detective Vasquez do before. I wondered if it was something they learned in detective training. Maybe it helped them think.

"You mean like the Longwell brothers? The bank robbers?"

"Exactly."

"What would they have to do with the case? You think they're connected? How could they figure in?"

"It looks like the Chao family is also the Longwell family."

He stopped bouncing and leaned forward, his forearms on his desk. "What? That doesn't make sense. How is that possible?"

"I haven't conclusively proved any of this, but it looks like Edward Chao's mother June wasn't a Wallace. She was a Longwell. Those Longwells."

"Whoa. Okay. Hold on. Edward Chao's mother, so Hannah's grandmother."

"That's right."

"She was part of the Longwell family?"

"Still is. She's still alive, and I'm pretty sure she is Horace Longwell's daughter."

"Whoa. Maybe that's a thing that could be a secret, something to know about the family, that you wouldn't want people to know."

"I think so."

"Yeah, yeah, that could be something. It could be."

"It could, and it might not be just that. Wasn't there some stolen money that was never recovered?"

"Oh yeah. There was a lot of it. Lots of money was never found."

"What if the Chao family got it, or at least some of it?"

"Whoa."

"It might injure your reputation if people knew you were descended from bank robbers, but it was three generations back, and you can't help who your great grandparents were. I don't know if that would be worth paying blackmail over, but what if your family rags to riches story, about hardworking immigrants gradually saving up enough to own a chain of restaurants, was really a story of inheriting stolen money, famous stolen money at that."

"You might be willing to pay a lot to stop that from coming out."

"I think you might. The thing is, who could have known about that, outside the family, and did the family even know? Did Hannah Chao know this about her family history? Had she always known? Had she recently found out? Did the blackmailer tell her?"

"Okay, wait a minute. Slow down a minute here. We need to start by finding out if it's true first. One step at a time. Okay? That's step one. Next comes the money. Can we prove the Longwells gave it to the Chaos?"

"I don't know if it's possible to prove either of those things, but do we really need to? I mean, if what we're looking for is something to blackmail over, does it really need to be proved? It just has to look bad enough for them not to want people to ask the question. A blackmailer wouldn't need actual definitive proof, just enough information that people would believe it."

"Yeah, it could be a motive anyway."

"It could be."

"I guess that's right, but then, wait a minute. So, someone finds this out, and tries to blackmail the Chaos, but which one of them? Hannah? Nina? Wait. You don't think Hannah was blackmailing her own family, do you?"

"No. I don't think so. I mean, I suppose it's possible, but no, that doesn't make sense. Wouldn't this information coming out hurt Hannah just as much? Wouldn't it hurt the whole family?"

"Right. Yeah, that doesn't make sense. Hannah wouldn't have been the blackmailer, but then who was, and how did Hannah end up murdered?"

"It could have been anyone who wanted money, which is pretty much anyone, and who could have found out about the Longwell connection, which, if Hannah knew about it, could have been anyone who had contact with Hannah."

"Hannah spent a lot of time with Nina on the movie set, and before that, when they were preparing. They were together a lot, so anyone working on the movie, anyone who might have been there, could have seen something, heard something."

"So, cast, crew, the assistant, that agent."

"Yeah, yeah, all those people. I've got all their names."

He leaned back in his chair again. "There's another possibility too, another angle. What if there was some conflict within the family. What if Hannah, or someone in the family, wanted to come clean about the Longwell money. They might have thought it was better to get ahead of it, if it might come out, cut the blackmailer off, remove the threat that way, or maybe they just felt guilty about it and wanted to tell the truth for that reason, get it off their chest, something like that."

"So we're back to the possibility that the blackmailer wasn't the killer. Then it could have been anyone in the family."

"Nina, Olivia, her husband Jake, even the parents. It's hard to imagine that, but it could have been an accident. Maybe they got in an argument and it got out of hand."

"It's possible."

"The whole thing still would have sprung from the blackmail though. Someone thought they could get money out of Hannah."

"Or out of someone else in the family. Maybe someone else received the note, and Hannah got it from them."

"Right. So which one was it? If you were the blackmailer, which member of the family would you approach?"

"Which member of the family has the most to lose?"

We looked at each other, and at the exact same time we both said, "Nina."

The detective stood up and reached for his jacket.

"I think it's time for another trip to that movie set."

CHAPTER 13

On Location

They were still shooting at the same location in Santa Monica, so the set and, within it, Nina's trailer, were easy to find. Detective Figueroa knocked on the trailer door. After a few seconds, the freckled face and voluminous hair of Lucy the assistant filled the doorway. She said nothing, but stood back and let us walk in.

Nina was sitting next to a small, built-in table, holding what appeared to be her script.

"I'm sorry to interrupt your work, Ms. Chao. Ms. Graepenteck and I just have a few questions to ask you."

"It's all right. Do you want to sit down?"

There wasn't much space in which to do so.

"That's not necessary. This won't take much time. We'd like to ask a few questions about your grandmother."

"We talked about my grandmother last time. I don't think I have anything to add."

The detective gave me a nod, and I took over the questioning.

"Not Rose Kahale. Your paternal grandmother."

I watched Nina as I said that, to see if she registered any discomfort with the subject. I didn't notice any, but she was supposed to be a pretty good actress.

"Grandma June? What would you like to know?"

"What do you know about her childhood?"

"That's a strange question, but okay."

She put the script down on the table and leaned back against the wall behind her.

"Um, let's see. She was born in New Hampshire, but then they moved out here to California when she was little. I'm pretty sure she doesn't even remember New Hampshire. I don't think I've ever heard her talk about it."

"Any siblings, or was it just her and her parents?"

"She's an only child. I don't understand this. Why are you asking about her?"

"Could we talk to your grandmother?"

"I wish you wouldn't. She's old, and she's sick, and I can't imagine she could tell you anything useful. I don't get why you want to know about her anyway."

Lucy the assistant cleared her throat, twice, and leaned forward, so that her head and all that hair came between me and Nina.

"Um, it's almost Nina's call time."

Nina glanced at her phone.

"That's right. I'm sorry I can't be more helpful, but you really have to go now."

Neither the detective nor I resisted. We stepped out of the trailer and headed back to the car.

"What do you think, Detective? I can't quite tell about her. She seemed genuinely confused, but she might be acting."

"I'm not sure either, but I think we need to talk to her grandmother."

"She really didn't want us to do that, did she?"

"Exactly. Let's go."

CHAPTER 14

Grandma June

R obert Chao had died many years earlier, but June Chao still lived in the three bedroom ranch style in Sherman Oaks where they had lived together for decades, albeit now with round-the-clock nursing care and a live-in housekeeper who also did the shopping and the cooking.

The housekeeper was named Matilda. She was an almost perfectly spherically shaped woman with a seemingly permanent smile. She thought Mrs. Chao would welcome visitors, even if they were the police.

"Not many people come here anymore. Just me and the nurses."

"What about her family?"

Matilda dropped her voice to a near whisper and touched my arm gently.

"Even them. On her birthday they come, and some holidays, but not regular."

"Her granddaughters don't come to see her?"

She shook her head.

"Never?"

Matilda shrugged.

"Sometimes maybe, but not often."

"Did anyone come to see her recently? Within the last month or so?"

She started to shake her head again, but then stopped.

"You know, there was once, a few weeks ago, maybe a month, the youngest girl, Hannah. She came by one afternoon, but she didn't stay long, less than an hour."

She dropped her voice even more, so I could barely hear her.

"She's dead, you know. She got killed, little Hannah. It's so sad."

I nodded sympathetically. "Will Mrs. Chao be able to answer our questions?"

"Oh sure. She needs her oxygen. It's the lung disease. She was a smoker, you know. So it can be hard for her to talk for a long time, unless she has the oxygen, but her mind, it's perfect. She's a sharp lady, Mrs. Chao."

Matilda knocked on a set of double doors, but didn't wait for a response before opening them, revealing a bright, tidy room dominated by an adjustable hospital bed and a row of oxygen tanks.

"Here are your visitors!"

At that, Matilda retreated, closing the double doors behind her.

Detective Figueroa started to introduce himself, but Mrs. Chao interrupted him.

"It's about time you showed up here."

Her voice tumbled through a cement mixer full of sharp rocks on its way out of her throat, and she was holding her oxygen mask at the ready, but she was easily comprehensible.

"You were expecting me?"

"I was expecting someone, the police. If you had waited much longer I would have tried to call you, but I was hoping I wouldn't have to go to the trouble of convincing you to come. No one listens to a sick old woman. I thought if whoever was investigating my granddaughter's death had half a brain they would eventually show up here. It looks like you do have at least half a brain."

She kept her oxygen mask in her right hand, but pointed at me with her left.

"Who are you? Are you police too?"

"I'm a consultant with the department. I'm a genealogist."

"A genealogist! Well then, maybe you have more than half a brain. Maybe I won't have to explain so much to you. Maybe you already know."

The detective noticed a wheeled stool by the wall and rolled it over next to the bed.

"Is it all right if I sit down."

Mrs. Chao waved her left hand in assent, and the detective sat close to her.

"Why don't you tell us what you think we need to know."

She took a deep breath through her oxygen mask, and at the same time gestured at me and at a chair on the other side of her bed, so I took a seat there.

"My granddaughter Hannah came here a couple of weeks ago. She doesn't come often, and she just showed up, in the middle of the afternoon, without calling first, so I knew it had to be for some unusual reason."

She breathed into the oxygen mask again.

"She'd been working for her sister Nina, helping with her acting ambitions, trying to find interesting stories to tell, in interviews, for publicity. She was researching the Chao family and the restaurants, and she went to one of those genealogy sites."

At this she pointed at me.

"Anyway, she'd been looking into my family, and she was confused. She couldn't find any record of my birth, and then she found some document that showed my parents but not me. I expect you found the same one."

She pointed at me again.

I nodded. "The 1940 census."

"That's it. She just wanted some clarification. Ordinarily I might have lied to her, but she seemed determined to find out the whole story, and I was tired of keeping the secret, so I told her the truth, that I was raised by my aunt, and why I was raised by my aunt."

"And why was that? Why were you raised by your aunt?"

The detective seemed to be treating this like a confession, making sure she actually said everything, and didn't just hint.

"Because my father was a notorious criminal, Horace Longwell, the bank robber. Is that what you want me to say? My parents, I mean Harold and Emily Wallace, they tried to hide it from me. When I was small I didn't know. We moved out here to get away from the Longwell family, but with a family that big, and that many people who know the truth, you can't hide it forever. I found out."

She took another hit of oxygen.

"I didn't tell anyone though. Not for a long time. Why would I tell anyone that? I never told my son, or my granddaughters, but Hannah, she was getting close to finding out, and she came here to ask for my help, so I told her."

"And how did she react to that information? Was she upset? Angry? Sad?"

"She was disappointed. She was hoping to find heartwarming stories about the Chao restaurants, and instead she found the Longwell brothers. She wasn't angry. She just wasn't sure how she was going to handle it, if she could keep the truth from coming out, if she should even try. She asked me if she should tell Nina."

"And what did you tell her?"

"I said she should. I said it wasn't worth the effort to keep it a secret anymore."

"And was she going to? To tell Nina, or anyone else?"

"When she left here she hadn't decided. She was still confused."

"But she hadn't talked to anyone about what she had found? The census page? You were the first person she discussed it with?"

"That's what she said."

"Did she say anything to you about having received a note?"

"No. Did she receive a note?"

"Did she say anyone had threatened her?"

"No. What's this about a note?"

"She was found with a note in her pocket."

"What sort of a note? What did it say?"

"I know about your family."

"No. She didn't say anything about that. That must have happened later. I think she would have told me about that."

"Well, that is very helpful information, and I appreciate your being so honest."

She just nodded, with the oxygen mask on her face.

"There is another thing I want to ask you about, a related thing, related to the Longwell brothers."

Mrs. Chao took the mask off her face and stared at the detective. For a solid five seconds she didn't move a muscle. Then, after taking another breath of oxygen, she spoke.

"You want to know about the money."

The detective nodded.

"Here's what I will tell you about the money. I want you to get this right. Do you have a tape recorder?"

"I can record what you say on my phone."

"Those phones. They do everything now. Okay. Start the recording thing on your phone."

He did.

"Let me see it."

He showed her that it was recording.

"Okay. Here's what I will say. My name is June Chao, formerly June Wallace, formerly June Longwell, daughter of Horace Longwell, and this is what I will say about the Longwell brothers and any supposed money."

She took another hit of oxygen.

"If there was any unrecovered money, and if some, or even all, of that unrecovered money somehow found its way to the only living child of any of the Longwell brothers, and if that money was used by that child as the capital to expand a family business, then it all happened so long ago and has been so thoroughly covered over by legitimate transactions that no one who investigated would ever be able to find any shred of proof."

She puffed on the oxygen again.

"And another thing, a very important thing. Is that thing still recording?"

He nodded and showed her that it was.

"The most important thing of all, is that if that were true, if there were any money, then that Longwell child, and that child's spouse, would never have told their children or grandchildren or any other relatives about it. No one, absolutely no one other than that child and that child's spouse would ever have had any knowledge of any illegal activity, none of which could be proven anyway. All right. You can stop recording now."

He did.

"Did you tell Hannah about the money?"

"There wasn't any money."

"If there had been money, would you have told Hannah about it?"

"Hannah was a smart girl. She could have figured out a lot of things."

There was a knock on the double doors and a young woman in nurse's whites came in.

"It's medication time. Also, Matilda tells me you've been here a while. I think Mrs. Chao is probably tired now."

"I'm perfectly fine, but I don't have anything else to tell you."

She did look very tired. The detective and I thanked her and quietly left, thanking Matilda on the way out.

CHAPTER 15

Secrets

As we pulled away from June Chao's house, I was glad Detective Figueroa was driving, because my mind was so preoccupied with a tumult of thoughts that I couldn't concentrate on anything else. Nevertheless, all I could think of to say was, "Well, that answers some questions."

"And brings up others."

"Yes. A lot of them."

The synapses in the detective's brain must have been crackling too, because suddenly he spoke in a rapid fire manner very different from his usual rambling pace.

"Okay. Let's review. So Hannah Chao's body was found on Olvera Street."

"Do we know for sure that she was killed there, on those rocks, or is it possible her body was moved there?"

"All indications are that she was killed there."

"So she was probably meeting someone there."

"Right. Most likely the person who sent her the note."

"I know about your family."

"Right. So, now we're pretty sure that means I know your family got their restaurant money from the Longwell brothers, who are your, what, cousins?"

"They would be the Chao sisters' great great uncles, or great granduncles. People use both terms."

"Okay. So, someone knows this, but Hannah only found out a few weeks ago."

"She may have had some general suspicions before that, that there was a secret, but she didn't know the specifics until her grandmother told her."

"Right, but someone else found out about it too."

"Yes, and it wouldn't do that person any good unless Hannah also knew about it. The note wouldn't make any sense if Hannah didn't know."

"Or Nina, or Hannah and Nina."

"Probably both of them. They were spending a lot of time together, and Hannah was working for Nina."

"Right. So who could have found out?"

"Anyone who looked hard enough. The records I found are all public. Hannah found the same census record I did."

"But she didn't find the rest. I think you're underestimating what you do. Not everyone would be able to find the information the way you did."

"Maybe not, but I doubt June told anyone else."

"No. They had to find it out some other way."

"Maybe from Hannah."

"That's more likely. She was confused about it. She might have wanted to talk it out with someone."

"Makes sense."

"Okay, so who would have wanted to use that information? Who had motive to blackmail the Chao family?"

"The obvious answer is someone who needed money."

"Or someone who wanted to hurt them. We don't actually have any evidence that there was money involved. It could have been someone who wanted to scare them, to make them worry about whether or not the truth would come out."

"That's a good point, and there's also the possibility you mentioned before, that there could have been dissension within the family about whether they should make the truth public."

"Right. Maybe Hannah and Nina weren't the only ones who knew. There's Olivia, and Jake, and the parents."

"And we still have the possibility of anyone involved with the film."

"Yeah, the cast, the crew, the assistant, the agent, all still suspects at this point."

"So we found the family secret, but we're still nowhere."

"That's about the size of it."

We were quiet for a while. I was reflecting on all those suspects and our inability to narrow down the list. He was probably doing the same thing.

There was another question that had been nagging at me though. It wasn't especially pertinent to the case, or at least not to the part of it I had been hired for, and I hadn't asked it before because the answer could be something the detective wouldn't want to tell me, or wasn't supposed to tell me, and I didn't want to put him in an awkward position, but it had kept bouncing around my head, and that silence seemed like such an invitation. I tried to leave him to continue his ruminations in peace, but finally the question overpowered me and made its way out of my mouth.

"I hope you don't mind if I ask, Detective, but why don't you have a partner?"

He laughed.

I was relieved that he didn't seem angry or insulted, but I hadn't expected him to find the question amusing. I was glad he started explaining. I didn't mind at all that he went back to his usual rambling.

"That's a common misconception, that detectives always work with partners. A lot of people expect that. I think it comes from TV and movies, from entertainment. They always seem to be in pairs in TV shows, and sometimes they are, like Vasquez and Roth. They're the first detectives you worked with right?"

I nodded.

"Yeah, and you probably expected that, so you thought the TV thing was true in real life, and then here's me by myself, with no partner, and you're surprised, but a lot of detectives work without a partner, especially if the budget is tight, and there are a lot of cases. Detectives can get spread pretty thin."

"I see."

He laughed again. "Did you think it was because I was some sort of lone wolf, or none of the other detectives wanted to work with me or something?"

"Not at all. I was just curious."

"Right. Well now you know."

"Yes. It is interesting, having worked with Detective Roth and Detective Vasquez, and now working with you, seeing the different approaches you have, and the different ways your minds work. I mean, I'm no expert, but you all seem to me to be very good at your job, and yet you don't all go about it the same way."

"Everyone has their own style."

"Exactly, but you all solve your cases."

"Well, we do our best. This one isn't solved yet."

"So, Detective, what's the next step?"

"That's a good question. When I get in this kind of a spot, where there is a lot of information and a lot of suspects and no clear direction to go, I find it helps to take a little break, let my brain reset. Then I go over all the information again, and usually things become clearer."

"I do the same thing when I get stuck, in genealogy research. Sometimes your brain just needs a rest."

"It sounds like your work is a lot like my work."

"Detective Roth told me that too."

"You know, you don't have to call us all Detective all the time. You can call me Joe."

"Really? It's not unprofessional?"

"Well, probably don't do it when we're talking to suspects, questioning people, but when we're in the car like this, why not?"

"I have been told that I have a tendency to be more formal than is necessary. I guess I could call you Joe, and you can call me Ella, at least when we're in the car. When we're in front of suspects, we can be Detective Figueroa and Ms. Graepenteck."

"Sounds good. It's a deal."

Chapter 16

The Agent

I was back in my house, relaxing on my overstuffed grass green sofa, giving my brain a chance to refresh itself, when my phone rang. The screen said it was Detective Figueroa. I had agreed to call him Joe, at least some of the time, but that didn't mean I was going to change his name in my contacts. I answered the call.

"Turn on the local news, right now. You'll want to see it."

I happened, most conveniently, to be facing my television, and to be within easy reach of the remote control, so I was able to find the broadcast he was talking about in a matter of seconds. I saw a woman in a neon green suit and handcuffs being put into a police car by a uniformed officer.

"You're kidding me."

"Can you believe it? It was a big surprise to me when I heard."

The woman was yelling, but a reporter's voice drowned out whatever it was she was trying to say. "Ms. Lychek is a top agent, with clients including Oscar winners Lucas Ronson and Natalie Forrest, as well as up-and-comers like Nina Chao. Shock is reverberating through the industry."

"Wow. What did she do? This can't be about the murder."

"Apparently she's been embezzling, stealing right and left from all her clients, for years."

"That's unexpected."

"I think I need to talk to her. Do you want to come?"

I did.

I was able to observe through the interrogation room mirror as Detective Figueroa interviewed Carol Lychek. Actually, at least at first, the interview was mostly with her lawyer.

The detective started with a very casual attitude.

"So, I'm not here about embezzlement. How much your client stole and who she stole it from is not my concern, unless it relates to my murder case. I doubt she knows anything that would be useful to me, but I like to be thorough, so I thought I'd give her a chance to show how cooperative she can be."

"What do you want to ask my client, Detective?"

"I want to know about any interactions she had with Hannah Chao, first of all."

Ms. Lychek and her lawyer whispered and nodded at each other, and then the lawyer nodded at the detective, which seemed to be a signal for him to go ahead with his questions.

"Did you ever meet with Hannah Chao?"

"I wouldn't say I met with her. She was there sometimes when I met with Nina Chao."

"Did you have any conversations with her?"

"Not much beyond basic hello how are yous. She took a strong interest in her sister's career, but she didn't talk a lot. She just sat there and glared."

"Why glared? She was angry?"

"She thought everyone was out to get Nina. She was always on the defensive, expecting attacks."

"Did she have good reason for that? Did Nina receive threats?"

"Nothing out of the ordinary. Everyone receives threats."

"Did she ever mention any specific threats? Any attempts at blackmail?"

"Blackmail? Of Nina Chao? I don't think so. Was there blackmail? What is there to blackmail Nina about?"

"Do you remember anything unusual, any time when Hannah seemed especially suspicious or defensive?"

"I don't think so. She was always the same. Although actually, now that you mention it, there was one day, a few weeks ago, she was sitting in my office with Nina, and I noticed she wasn't glaring as much as usual. Her attention wasn't focused. She seemed preoccupied. I didn't really care, but Nina noticed it too, and when the meeting was over, she asked her about it."

"Nina asked Hannah about her attention not being focused?"

"She asked her what was wrong with her, and Hannah said something about having been to see their grandmother. I took a call and I didn't hear the rest of it, but they both got pretty worked up."

"You didn't hear anything else they said? Just that Hannah had seen their grandmother?"

"No. I wasn't paying attention. I just saw them get worked up, and then Nina grabbed Hannah's arm and sort of dragged her out the door."

"Dragged her?"

"Not in a violent way. It looked like she was telling her to shut up. The body language was sort of, let's not talk about this here, you know? Shut up and tell me later."

"Did they often have that kind of disagreement, get agitated with each other?"

"No. I think that was the only time I saw anything like that. Most of the time they were a team, presented a united front."

"A front? Did you get the sense they argued privately, when other people weren't around?"

"Oh I don't know, but they were sisters. Don't all sisters fight sometimes?"

"After that argument in your office, when was the next time you saw Hannah?"

"I don't know. She was usually on the set with Nina. I probably saw her there."

"Do you remember any other arguments, any agitation on the set?"

"Not really. The atmosphere might have been a little more prickly after that."

"What do you mean?"

"Well, now that I think about it, that argument might have been more serious than I thought. They did seem to be on each other's nerves a little after that, just things not as smooth between them. There was, I don't know, tension."

"Did they ever discuss it? Did you get any idea what the tension was about?"

"No. I didn't really notice it at the time. It's only in remembering that day now that I even thought of it."

"So you never heard either of them say anything about blackmail? Threats? A note?"

"A note? What note? There was a note?"

"Okay. Thanks for your cooperation. I'll make sure the detective on your case is made aware."

Detective Figueroa left the interrogation room and came into the observation room. He shrugged as he sat down next to me.

"It wasn't much. I had hopes for more."

"We have some new information though. Now we know Hannah talked to Nina about seeing June."

"But we don't know how much she told her."

"She told her enough to cause tension between them, enough tension that it was noticeable to other people. People who weren't as self-absorbed as the embezzling agent might have noticed more."

"That's true. People on the set might have noticed, other members of the cast, crew, that assistant, Lucy. She might have noticed something. Maybe someone overheard something useful. No one said anything in preliminary questioning, but I didn't have something specific to ask about then. I guess I need to go back to the set again."

CHAPTER 17

Divide and Conquer

I was about to go with Detective Figueroa to question people on the movie set when I got a surprising phone call. It was from Olivia Chao Lawrence.

"There are things the police probably should know, about my family, and I want to be honest, but it makes me nervous, telling an actual detective. I thought that maybe I could tell you though, if it was just you. A genealogist is somehow less intimidating than a detective."

"Okay. Do you want me to come to your house?"

"That would be good, if you could."

"All right. I think I do need to check with the detective, to make sure that's okay, for me to talk to you without him. Let me ask him, and I'll get right back to you."

I hung up and looked at the detective. "So I guess you heard that."

"Olivia wants you to come to her house?"

"Did you catch that bit about a genealogist being…"

"Less intimidating than a detective? Yeah, I'm not sure that's true, in general, but if that's how she feels, it works for me. If it makes her more comfortable, just talking to you, we'll get more information. You can go to her house, and I'll go to the film set, and then we'll meet up. We'll compare notes."

"It's a plan then."

The detective drove off. I called Olivia back to tell her I was on my way, and then I headed to the Valley.

The outside of the Lawrence house looked just as charming as the first time, and the inside just as dull and yet remarkably tidy. We sat in the living room again, and Jake kept the children out of the way again. Olivia was not nearly as relaxed as she had been when the previous conversation had begun, but not quite as tense as she had been when it ended.

"The first thing I want to tell you, just so you understand, is, you know my sisters and I had a pop group, Brite, years ago."

"Yes."

"And, when you get a little fame, things can happen. People can be crazy, sometimes threatening."

"Yes."

"We needed security. Sometimes we had stalkers."

"I'm sure."

"Well I had a very scary one, really dangerous."

"Oh, I'm sorry."

"Nothing ever happened. It was just threats, and he got caught, eventually, and put in jail, but still, it was frightening."

"Of course."

"I don't want to go into the details, but it made me not want that kind of notoriety again. I just, I was done. I didn't want to do it anymore."

"I can understand that."

"Well my sisters, they said that too, that they understood, but I don't know if they really did. It didn't make them stop wanting to be famous, more famous, and they kept telling me I needed to get over it, and, well, we were never really as close after that, and that's not the only reason why, but it's a big part of it, and now, I'll never talk to Hannah again, and it's just an added piece of the grief."

She grabbed a tissue from a full box on the table next to her, but she managed to stop any tears from flowing.

"I'm telling you this because you need to know about it, the background, what happened before, so you will understand why what happened later was so strange."

It sounded like she had prepared a series of talking points, and I didn't want to interrupt her narrative flow, so I just stayed silent and listened.

"A few days before she died, Hannah called me. She said she wanted to come and talk to me about something, something about our family history. It was so surprising. She so rarely called me about anything anymore, and this was such a strange topic, not something we would normally talk about, at least not something that would be such a big deal. She said she wanted to talk to me about it in person, not on the phone. We made plans. She was going to come here and tell me about whatever it was. She said she was going to try to get Nina to come too, but Nina didn't want to talk about it, so she didn't think she could get her to come. It was all so mysterious and confusing. I really tried to get her to tell me what it was, but she just wouldn't, and then..."

She grabbed another tissue, and this time she did press it briefly against her right eye.

"And then she was killed, and I felt from the beginning that it must have something to do with whatever she wanted to tell me, and then the detective showed up here with you, with a genealogist, and, well, it was all so overwhelming."

She dabbed at her eyes again.

"I was wondering, hoping, really, since you're investigating our family, do you have any idea what it was, what she wanted to tell me?"

So that was it, the reason she had asked me to come alone. She thought I had genealogical information she wanted. Well, she was right. I did, and I saw no reason not to tell her so, although I thought there was a better source for the details.

"I think I do. It's about your grandmother, June Chao, and I think you should probably ask her to explain it. She talked to your sister Hannah about it, and she talked to Detective Figueroa and me about it, and I'm sure she would happily tell you all about it, probably much more than she told us."

"Really? It's about Grandma June? It's not something terrible, is it?"

"I've certainly come across much worse."

"Okay. I'll ask her about it. Even if it's not too terrible, it is what got Hannah killed, isn't it?"

"It does seem to be a factor, at least. Are you sure she didn't tell you anything about it? She didn't let any detail slip, even though she wanted to wait and talk about it in person?"

"She wouldn't tell me anything. I really tried."

"Did she mention anything about a note?"

"No. Someone sent her a note? Was someone threatening her? Someone was! That's what she meant! She said, 'I don't want to tell you now, because you'll overreact.' Someone had threatened her, and she thought I would freak out if she told me. I probably would have, and it turns out it would have been the right reaction. I wish she had told me. If I freaked out, and called the police, which is probably what she didn't want me to do, well then."

It was getting harder for her to keep from crying. I asked her one more time if she could think of anything else Hannah said. She shook her head, and then I left her with her box of tissues.

CHAPTER 18

Other Avenues

I called Detective Figueroa from my car, but only got his voicemail. It was several hours later when he finally returned my call.

"How was your trip to the movie set?"

"I never got there." He sounded very tired.

"What happened?"

"Remember how I said detectives can end up spread pretty thin? I got another murder case."

"And now you have to work on both cases at the same time?"

"Right, and I had to go to the crime scene and do all the preliminary work."

"I see."

"How was your interview with Olivia?"

"I don't think she was involved, in the murder or in the blackmail. Her issue with her family has to do with a frightening experience she had with a stalker, and her not wanting to be famous anymore. The most important bit of information she gave me was that Hannah called her a few days before she was killed, wanting to talk to her about their family history."

"After she talked to their grandmother."

"Exactly. So, if Olivia is telling the truth, then Hannah did want to discuss the Longwell connection with other members of the family."

"We could check the phone records. That can't tell us what they said, but it can prove whether or not Hannah called her."

"She might have called their parents too."

"Right. Maybe she did. I can also check that."

"Olivia said she couldn't get Hannah to tell her what specifically she wanted to talk about, just that it was about their family history, but it seems pretty clear that Hannah and Nina discussed it in more detail, even argued about it."

"Right. So Nina is still a suspect."

"I think so."

"I need to question her again, but right now I have more urgent things to do for this other case."

"Of course."

"There are still a lot of other suspects, too."

"About that, I have an idea for something I might do, while you're doing those urgent things."

"What's that?"

"I didn't mention this before, because it was outside my remit of researching the Chao family history, and because I thought it might raise conflict of interest issues, but if it doesn't break any rules, I could talk to someone who might be able to shine some light on possible suspects working on the film, any problems there, such as the protesters Lucy the assistant mentioned."

The detective said he thought it was a good idea, so I steeled myself to make at least one uncomfortable phone call. I was going to try to get an appointment to see Nicholas de Brisay III.

Chapter 19
Family Reunion

Getting an appointment proved to be much less difficult than I expected. I found myself feeling a little disappointed at how anticlimactic it was when the receptionist, or whoever she was, the woman who answered the phone, scheduled me in without my even having to explain much about what I wanted. I just said that I was a relative of his and a genealogist and I had some questions to ask him, and I got the appointment.

His office was, of course, at the top of a tall building, with broad views of the city, but when I walked inside it, I didn't think of flying, or being on top of a mountain. Instead, I thought immediately of a zoo. It wasn't just that the room was both wide enough for elephants and tall enough for giraffes, or that some of the many photos on the walls contained animals from multiple continents, including what were probably endangered species. It was that the aim of the whole arrangement seemed to be to compel the visitor to look at everything, and to be amazed.

Within the first ten seconds after entering the room, I knew that Nicholas de Brisay III had been many places and won many accolades. Each certificate, plaque, and statuette was highlighted in its own particular way, and the photos with the most recognizable people and places in them were in easy view. I imagined an office decoration process in which an expensive, well-known-in-certain-circles interior designer implemented a strategic plan to exacting specifications, closely supervised along the way.

The man himself was no less carefully arranged. His suit jacket hung on a padded wooden hanger from a peg on the wall near the desk. It and his pants were a vibrant blue, about halfway between royal and navy. His shirt was also blue, but so pale it was almost white, with dark blue vertical stripes so narrow as to be nearly imperceptible. Its cuffs were neatly rolled, just twice, enough to show an undoubtedly extremely expensive watch.

I was trying to decide whether the main color of his tie was dark blue or purple when he spoke to me, snapping my gaze to his face. I saw then how he chose the color of his suit. It almost exactly matched his eyes. His hair was very dark, and his skin was of that leathery texture considered ruggedly attractive in men, and ruggedly unattractive in women. The overall effect was of two of those fancy blue and white porcelain teacups on an antique oak table. It was so absorbing that it took me a moment to register what he had said.

"Your mother is Patricia de Brisay?"

"Patricia de Brisay Graepenteck, yes."

He moved a few feet closer to me, examining my face, forehead to chin, then cheekbone to cheekbone, as he sailed past a chair and a small table, without looking at them and without any fear of stubbing a toe or banging a knee.

"How is she, your mother?"

The words were gracious, solicitous even, as was the facial expression, but something in the manner made me feel as if I were looking up at a praying mantis about to devour me.

"She is well, thank you."

"I remember meeting you, when you were very young."

"Do you? I have only the vaguest recollection."

"You were a smart little girl. I remember that. You were observant."

"Was I?"

"You watched everybody. You noticed everything. I expect you still do."

I shrugged.

"You're a genealogist now?"

"Yes."

"Have you done research on the de Brisay family?"

"Of course. I think all genealogists begin with their own families."

"Found anything interesting?"

"Everything about my family is interesting to me."

He showed me his teeth. I wouldn't exactly call it a smile, but he changed the arrangement of his face, and I could see that he'd had a lot of straightening and whitening done.

"Are you here to ask me genealogy questions, or is this a social call? Are you and Patricia going to start attending family events again?"

"I admit my primary motive is professional, but it's only obliquely related to genealogy. I'm not here about the de Brisay family."

I noticed a slight reduction in tension in the muscles around his intensely blue eyes.

"Then why are you here?"

"I've been hired by the LAPD, as a consultant, to do some research connected to the death of Hannah Chao. I expect you're aware of the case."

"I see."

"It's possible she was murdered for some reason related to her family, but it's also possible, given that she was found on Olvera Street, and that she was working for her sister Nina, that it was for some reason connected to the film Nina is working on. I thought your perspective, as an executive producer on the film, might be valuable. You might have an idea who might have had a motive to kill Hannah Chao."

"And you thought coming here on your own, without the police, might make me more likely to open up."

"Actually, I thought it was an opportunity to talk to you. I was, frankly, curious. I haven't had any contact with any of the de Brisays since I was a small child. My mother has her opinions, and her reasons for them, and I have no cause to doubt her, but that doesn't stop me from thinking, from time to time, about finding out for myself."

"So it's curiosity that brought you here?"

"Not only curiosity, but yes."

"And what's your impression so far?"

"I haven't had time to gain an impression."

"That's not the observant little Ella I remember."

"Maybe I've lost the knack."

"I doubt it, but maybe you've also developed more circumspection."

"Would you mind if I asked you a few questions about Hannah Chao, and the cast and crew of Sterling?"

"What would you like to know?"

"Did you know Hannah? Do you know Nina?"

"I've never met either of them."

"Do you have any idea who might wish to harm them?"

"None whatsoever."

"Are you aware of any conflicts involving either of them? Arguments with coworkers, with the director, with any of the producers?"

"No."

"Are you aware of any group that is protesting the film, that objects to its being made?"

"There is some group that was making a fuss about... something. I don't remember the name of the group or what exactly they claimed their problem was, but I know it's been dealt with. All they wanted was some publicity."

"I gather your approach as an executive producer on Sterling has not been very hands on."

"Not at all. It's purely an investment."

"Are any of the other executive producers more involved in the production?"

"Well the two stars, Stephanie Warrick and Jack Laraby, are executive producers, so they are involved, but their actual production work, from what I hear, is mostly limited to concerns over the quality and location of their trailers, and how much time they will spend on screen."

"And from whom do you hear this?"

"From Jennifer More and Julia Kazinsky, the producers. They keep the executive producers more or less up to date on the progress of the production."

"So they would be the people to ask about what actually happens on set?"

"Better than me, at least."

"So do the rest of the executive producers get their information from those two?"

"I would expect so, although a few of them have children working on the production, so they may hear stories from them."

"Who has children on the production?"

He sighed and leaned against a nearby armchair.

"Maybe not children, but relatives. Martin Hellenberg's granddaughter is a PA, that's a production assistant, someone who gets coffee and picks up dry cleaning."

"Yes, I know what a PA is."

"Louis Rouleau's grandson or stepson or something is too, I think. That may be it. Oh, Reggie Moss said he got a niece a job as someone's assistant, one of the actors. I don't remember which one."

I hoped my recognition of the name didn't register on my face.

"So are the executive producers all friends?"

He stared at me, giving me that praying mantis feeling again.

"We tend to move in similar circles."

"Do you think any of them are likely to know anything about Hannah or Nina Chao, anything that might be helpful for the investigation?"

"I couldn't say."

"All right, well, thank you for answering my questions."

"So that's it then? We're not going to have a personal chat? Catch up on all these lost years? You don't want to stay and have a drink with me?"

I felt no need to acknowledge his sarcasm.

"I'm afraid I have a meeting to get to, but I appreciate your giving me this time."

I turned and headed for the door. As I closed it behind me, he called out, "I'll look forward to seeing you at the next family event."

CHAPTER 20

Friends and Family

I called Detective Figueroa to give him an update.

"Anything good? Any new information?"

"I don't think so, nothing useful, although I found out how Lucy got her job as Nina's assistant."

"Oh? How?"

"Her uncle is one of the executive producers. I do wonder if her being hired was part of the negotiation for Nina's getting the role, or if it happened afterward, but I doubt it really matters."

"Hmm. Yeah. I'm trying to think of a way that might make her a more likely suspect, give her a motive for killing Hannah, but I'm drawing a blank, just nothing, nada."

"I can't think of anything either. Unless..."

"What?"

"No. I had this fleeting idea about some convoluted way in which Lucy got the job by blackmailing Nina, but why? If her uncle is an executive producer, she wouldn't need any more leverage than that."

"Right. Yeah, and I was thinking something real farfetched about what if there was some way Nina manipulated her way into getting the role, but then why would Lucy need the job as her assistant, or even want it, unless she was there to keep an eye on her, but then why would that be necessary, if her uncle is in charge? No, it doesn't work. It doesn't make sense."

"So, what do we do now? I can try to find out if there are any more Chao family secrets, but I doubt it."

"Right. You can look, you can try, but I think we found the secret the note was about, what the blackmailing was for."

"Maybe we just leave it alone for a few hours, get a good night's sleep, let our subconscious minds mull it over again."

"Yeah. Maybe we see if we have any ideas tomorrow."

I did look into the Chao family some more, just in case there was something else. I researched Christina Morales Chao's father's family, because she and Edward hadn't wanted to discuss that branch either, but I found nothing unusual at all, just people with ordinary families and ordinary jobs.

I was feeling frustrated, and I thought it might be worthwhile to get Cormac Roth's input, so I called him.

"You're not in the middle of anything, are you?"

"Not really. I'm in the car with Raf, but we're just going back to the station to do paperwork."

"I could use any suggestions from either of you. Detective Figueroa and I still have too many suspects, and none of them seem all that likely. Besides, he's got another case now, so he can't put his full attention on this one."

"All right. I'll put you on speaker. Tell us what you've got."

I did.

"No useful fingerprints on the note?"

"Only Hannah's."

"Phone records didn't help?"

"They confirmed calls we already knew about, but didn't show any new ones."

I heard Detective Vasquez speaking in the background, but couldn't make out many of the words.

"I didn't quite catch that."

"Raf says you need to talk to someone who knows the family but isn't in the family, like a longtime neighbor or coworker. You need a different perspective on the family dynamics, to sort out the conflicts among the sisters and figure out how deep they go."

"That's a great idea!"

"Yeah, he gets them sometimes."

"And I think I might know how I could find someone like that."

"Good! Glad we could help."

"Thanks, Raf. Thanks, Mac."

"Hey! Well done!"

"I'm getting the hang of it."

"Are you sure you've never had a nickname?"

"I've always just been Ella."

"I guess we'll stick with that then, for now."

It wasn't hard to get Aunt Louisa and Aunt Agatha to agree to lunch at my mother's house the next day, even though it meant they both had to rearrange their schedules. A perk of being the closest thing either of them has to a grandchild is that they tend to be delighted with any chance to see me. I convinced my mother to host by promising both to supply the food, from one of her favorite restaurants, and to do the dishes afterward.

We ate in the dining room. Somehow, when Aunt Louisa is involved, eating in the kitchen seems inappropriate. Maybe she's to blame for this tendency some people seem to think I have for being overly formal.

My mother uses the dining room so rarely that she has never bothered to redecorate it. Its walls are still oak paneling on the bottom half and hunter green wallpaper on the top, their forestlike darkness broken up only by two windows on one of them and large portraits of all the Patrick de Brisays, Senior, Junior, III, and IV, one on each wall. My grandfather, Patrick IV, is between the two windows.

We had barely begun our meal when Aunt Agatha declared herself unable to restrain her curiosity any longer.

"What is it you wanted to talk to us about? Is it the murder case you're working on?"

"Actually it is, or at least it's related to that."

"Oh good! I knew it! Didn't I say so, Lou?"

"You did, Dear, and I agreed with you. How can we help, Ella? You know we will do anything we can."

"I do know that, and I appreciate it. What I need is for all three of you to tap into your knowledge of Los Angeles history and Los Angeles families. I want you to tell me any stories you have ever heard about the Chao family, of Chez Chao restaurants."

My mother looked up at the ceiling, as if there were information written up there. "Chez Chao. That's that Asian fusion place. There are five or six of them, but they're fancier than the typical chain. Each one is a little different, I think."

Aunt Louisa nodded. "Yes, yes, that's right. The one in Pasadena has a certain Hawaiian flair, or at least they have some dishes that feature pineapple. That's the one Rose Morales took a particular interest in. You remember Rose, Aggie? Her daughter married into the Chao family."

"Of course! She was fun, lots of energy. She was on that museum committee."

"You knew Rose Kahale Morales?" I tried to sound more surprised than I really was. Aunt Louisa knows and remembers a bewildering number of people.

"Yes, Darling, but not terribly well. We were on that committee together for a while, and we used to run into each other at events. We were more acquaintances than friends, but Aggie is absolutely correct. Rose had a tendency to raise the energy level of even the most boring procedural meeting. Did you ever meet her, Patricia?"

"I don't think so."

I didn't want the topic to drift, so I interjected. "Did she ever talk about the Chaos?"

"I'm sure she did, but nothing she said about them particularly springs to mind."

Aunt Agatha hurriedly finished chewing a mouthful of pasta. "Her grandchildren had that singing group!"

"Oh yes, Aggie, right again. She had three granddaughters and they formed a little girl group. They had some significant success, as I recall."

"Yes. It was called Brite. I know about that. They still have some pretty serious fans who call themselves

Briters. The eldest daughter, Nina, is an actress now. She has a part in a big studio film called Sterling."

Aunt Louisa put down her fork, the mouthful she had been about to eat still on it, and Aunt Agatha increased her chewing speed again.

"Sterling? We were just discussing that the other day, weren't we, Aggie?"

Aunt Agatha nodded vigorously.

"It's one of those biography pictures, about Christine Sterling. They had a setback in filming because of that incident on Olv..." Aunt Louisa turned toward Aunt Agatha for a moment and then stared at me. "That's your case, isn't it? The murder on Olvera Street! Oh, that is exciting!"

"I don't really want to get into the details of the case."

"Of course not, but we were just discussing that with Julia Moss. Her husband is one of the executive producers. Oh, she went on and on about it!"

This time I was the one to put down my fork, and my knife. In fact, I lost interest in my food altogether. "Who is Julia Moss?"

"Oh, you wouldn't be interested in her. She has nothing to do with the Chao family."

"You never know, Aunt Louisa. The most surprising things can prove useful sometimes. Please tell me about her."

"Well, if you insist."

"Yes, please."

"All right then. Her husband is Reggie Moss. Reggie and his brother Wally are entertainment lawyers, and reasonably successful at it, I understand, but the real money comes from Julia. She's a Haverville. You know, the real estate Havervilles, absolutely drowning in money. She's the reason Reggie can indulge himself in things like investing in film production. He just loves being able to call himself an executive producer."

"Julia likes the title too."

"That's a good point, Aggie. She does indeed. She kept calling the movie 'Reggie's latest project' as if he were solely responsible for it, and she must have said the words 'executive producer' four or five times."

"At least."

"Yes. I understand it causes a bit of resentment in the Moss family, Julia giving Reggie all that money to play with."

"How so?"

"Well, Darling, the brothers, Reggie and Wally, they work together, partners in the law firm, and I understand they are quite close. In fact, I don't think it upsets Wally particularly, Julia's money. It's his wife. What's her name, Aggie?"

"Eleanor."

"That's right. Eleanor Moss. I don't think I've ever met her. Have you met her, Aggie?"

Aunt Agatha shook her head.

"But according to Julia, her sister-in-law Eleanor is quite resentful. It seems she comes from a family that had some sort of catastrophic business failure, from which they never recovered, somewhere Back East, and, this is Julia's opinion, you understand, but she claims that Eleanor thinks of herself as someone who was destined for wealth, but had it stolen from her, almost as if she were deposed royalty. Julia probably exaggerates, but what is true is that she and her sister-in-law do not get along, and Julia is convinced that her money is the reason."

I sat staring at my still nearly full plate, processing what Aunt Louisa had said, and trying to figure out how it could be relevant to Hannah Chao's murder. I felt certain, deep in my gut, that it was important, but I couldn't come up with any logical connection.

Aunt Agatha scraped the last bit of pasta from her plate and put it into her mouth. She put down her fork and chewed, less hurriedly than before. When she had finished, she announced, "It was banking."

Aunt Louisa turned toward her. "What's that, Dear?"

"The catastrophic business failure, Eleanor Moss. The family business was banking."

"Aggie, you are absolutely hitting every nail today. That's right. They were a family of bankers, in one of those little tiny states."

"New Hampshire."

"Is that right? Are you sure?"

"Oh yes Lou, I'm positive. It was New Hampshire."

CHAPTER 21

The Soundstage

I managed to pay attention to at least half of what was said during the rest of the lunch, and I kept my promise to do the dishes, but as soon as I got home I did some research on the Moss family, or rather on the Withings family. Eleanor Moss had been born a Withings, in a little town called Blueford, New Hampshire.

It wasn't so much the genealogy records that interested me, although I did map out Eleanor's family tree. It was easy to do quickly. New Hampshire happens to be one of the few states for which many detailed records are readily available online. What had my curiosity at an especially high level, however, was the possibility of finding old newspaper articles about the family, specifically about what the aunts had called their catastrophic business failure.

That took a little more digging, but it wasn't all that difficult, as the tribulations of the Withings family made the news throughout New England. Once I had the facts, I called Detective Figueroa.

"They were in banking? In New Hampshire?"

"And guess what happened to them and their banking business."

"I'm guessing they got robbed."

"Their bank was in fact the very first bank to be robbed by the Longwell brothers."

"The first one?"

"And it was a disaster. It ruined them."

"Whoa."

"I'm thinking that was probably something Lucy the assistant knew about."

"Looks like another trip to the movie set."

They were finished with the park location in Santa Monica, which was good timing on their part, because the news that Hannah Chao was the Olvera Street murder victim was now out. The Briters were both heartbroken and outraged, and they made this known not only on social media, but also in pilgrimages to Olvera Street. They had decided that the film was somehow to blame for Hannah's death, and so had also organized small but loud protests at any location they associated with the production. As filming was now being done on a soundstage, the primary site of these protests was currently outside the main gate of the studio lot.

The efforts of the Briters made the story bigger than it otherwise would have been, so both Olvera Street and the studio lot were also focal points for all the entertainment news shows and sites, and several new podcasts had been created, mostly focused on the murder itself, although some were more concerned with Brite and its loyal fans, or with the film and its subject. All of that meant that approaching the studio gate required dodging people, signs, and cameras, which took some time. Once we were through it, however, we were guided to the correct soundstage with no difficulty, and as filming was not actually in progress at that moment, the detective's badge was all we needed to be able to talk to Nina Chao.

She was sitting with Anthony Kells. The two of them were apparently the main players in the scene that would soon start filming. They seemed preoccupied with each other, and neither of them noticed us until we were nearly in their laps.

"Oh hello. Look, Tony, it's the police again. What can we do for you today, Detective? You know, between making details of my sister's death public and arresting my agent, you haven't exactly been making my life easier."

"I know. This must all be very difficult. We did our best to keep your sister out of the news. It's just impossible to keep something like that quiet for long. As for your agent, well, that was out of my hands completely. I'm a homicide detective. Embezzlement is not my department."

"Yes, well, I know you're just doing your job, but what could you possibly still have questions about?"

"Actually, at the moment, we're looking for your assistant."

"For Lucy? She's around here somewhere. She's supposed to be bringing me some water. Why do you need to talk to her?"

I looked around and quickly picked out that distinctive freckled face, just a few yards away and closing fast. I nudged the detective and pointed my chin in her direction. He turned that way and saw her. Nina's attention was pulled as if by gravity back into Tony's orbit. He granted her the exact same smile I remembered from our previous visit to the set. I expected his mirror had witnessed diligent practice.

Lucy was holding a bottle of water in each hand. She handed one to Nina and kept the other for herself.

"Hello Ms. Moss."

"Hello Detective. Do you have more questions for Nina?"

"Actually, you're the one I really need to talk to right now."

"Me?"

"Is there someplace quieter? more private?"

"I guess so, if Nina doesn't mind."

Nina waved her hand dismissively.

We followed Lucy through an obstacle course of people and equipment until we reached a door that led from the dark interior of the soundstage to the bright sunlight outside. We went around a corner where the enormous building blocked the sun and created a pocket of shade. It was just as busy out there as it had been inside, but all the people were passing by us, back and forth, several yards away. No one was standing still, or in a position to eavesdrop for more than a few seconds. Lucy picked a spot near the wall and turned to face us.

"What can I do for you?"

"What does the name Longwell mean to you?"

Her eyes opened wide and her skin turned bright pink. She shifted her feet and plunged her right hand into the pocket of her jeans. Her left hand still held the water bottle.

"What do you mean?"

"Did you ever hear Nina or her sister Hannah mention the name Longwell?"

Lucy chewed on the inside of her cheeks.

"I don't think so. I mean, I don't remember hearing them say that name."

"Do you remember a day a few weeks ago when Hannah came to see Nina, after having been to see their grandmother?"

"Their grandmother? I don't think so. At least I don't remember anything like that, but I wouldn't listen to their private conversations, so even if they talked about something, about that name you mentioned, or anything else, I wouldn't know."

"Right. I'm sure you're always very professional, very good at your job, but, I mean, we're all human, right? I'm sure you didn't intend to overhear anything, but you probably heard at least a few words, especially if their voices were raised, if they were arguing."

Lucy chewed on her lips and rocked back and forth on her heels. Then she pulled her phone out of her pocket.

"Would you like to call someone, Ms. Moss?"

She grasped her phone tightly, probably in an attempt to disguise the fact that her hands were shaking. She put the bottle of water under her arm so she could get both hands onto her phone. She kept shaking though, and soon the bottle dropped and hit the ground. She left it there and worked the phone with her thumbs.

"I don't think I should answer any more questions until I talk to a criminal lawyer. I don't actually have one, but I'm sure my uncle does, so that's who I'm calling. You probably didn't realize, I mean I know Moss is a common name, but Reggie Moss, the executive producer, he's my uncle."

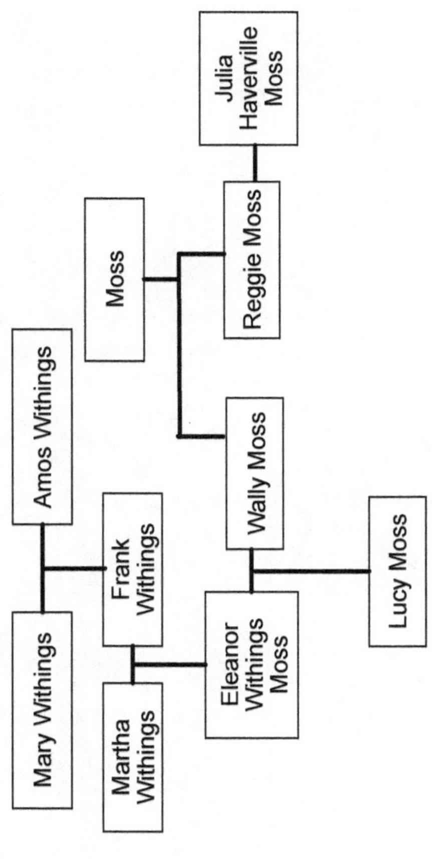

Julia Haverville Moss
Moss
Reggie Moss
Amos Withings
Wally Moss
Mary Withings
Frank Withings
Martha Withings
Eleanor Withings Moss
Lucy Moss

CHAPTER 22

The Executive Producer

Calling her uncle didn't initiate the rescue operation that Lucy seemed to think it would, but after several telephone conversations, some involving her parents, and some involving a law firm, negotiations resulted in Lucy's being seated in an interrogation room. Next to her was a young woman who couldn't have been more than a year or two out of law school, and across from them both was Detective Figueroa. I watched the proceedings through the mirror from the room next door.

I couldn't see the detective's face, only the back of his head, and for the first few minutes he said absolutely nothing. He spent that time moving papers around, scribbling notes on a yellow legal pad, taking sips of water. When he finally did speak, his tone was solicitous.

"Are you thirsty? Would you like some water? A soda?"

The lawyer refused the offer. Lucy crossed her arms and sighed.

"If you want something, just let me know."

"I want to go home."

The lawyer reminded Lucy that she didn't have to say anything, but Lucy just stared at the detective, and didn't acknowledge the warning.

He scribbled again.

She sighed again.

Finally he put all his papers into one stack, and laid them next to the legal pad.

"So, Ms. Moss, how did you find out that Nina and Hannah Chao were descended from the Longwell brothers?"

Her eyes opened wide for a second, registering mild surprise, but she quickly recovered herself and went back to her previous attitude of annoyed boredom. "What are you talking about?"

"Did you overhear them talking about it, or did you do research on your own, discover it for yourself?"

She tightened her crossed arms and stared at him.

"No, you didn't do the research, or at least, that's not how you found out. Maybe you looked up a few things after you heard them talking. Yes, that's it."

He started scribbling again.

"What are you writing down? I didn't say anything."

"So, you overheard them talking, maybe in the trailer, or somewhere on the set? Hannah had been to see her grandmother, and she was telling Nina what she'd learned, and that was a shock to you, wasn't it? You didn't expect that at all. You had no idea they had any connection to the Longwell brothers, but you were very familiar with them, weren't you? You had heard about them your whole life. Do you want to tell me why?"

She chewed her bottom lip.

"No? It's because your mother is from New Hampshire, right? And not just that, her family owned a bank, right? And not just any bank, but the very first bank the Longwell brothers robbed. That's right, isn't it?"

The pale skin under Lucy's freckles was turning red, and her eyes were getting shiny.

"And it ruined them. It ruined their reputation. No one trusted their security, and they lost out to competitors, and that was it, right? They were going to be rich, but then the Longwell brothers destroyed that dream, didn't they, and your mother's family never forgot, and you grew up knowing that the Longwell family crushed your family's dreams, just crushed them into little pieces."

Lucy was starting to sniffle.

"So when you heard Hannah telling Nina that Horace Longwell was their great grandfather, and that the money they always thought the Chao family saved up, little by little, working in restaurants, the money that turned that one little barely surviving restaurant into two and then three and then four, that started them up that economic ladder, that made it possible for the Chao sisters to be famous, and for Nina Chao to have this important role in this movie, to be your boss, that money was stolen money, stolen from your family. That money that they had, it should have been yours. That money rightfully belonged to you."

Tears were falling now, and her nose was running. The detective handed her a box of tissues. The lawyer looked at the tissues, and then at Lucy, but didn't say anything.

"It wasn't fair, was it? You had begged your uncle to help you out, your uncle with the rich wife, who had the power to help you get your foot in the door. You had debased yourself, begging for a job being ordered around by this wannabe moviestar, because one day you are going to be someone with that kind of power, right? One day, you are going to be in charge, but you have to climb your way up, and when you heard that Nina Chao was in that position, that she was your boss, because of stolen money, money that was rightfully yours, well that was just too much, wasn't it? You couldn't just let that go. You had to do something!"

Sobs burst from Lucy. She was pulling tissues from the box, and piling up the used ones next to it.

"It isn't fair! It isn't right! I had to make it right!" The lawyer made impotent attempts at calming Lucy. The detective ignored them.

"So you wrote the note."

"I'm not a criminal. I didn't plan to do anything wrong. I really didn't!"

"But you gave Hannah the note."

She shook her head.

"Not Hannah. Nina. I meant it for Nina."

The lawyer tried once more to get Lucy to be quiet, and then resigned herself to failure.

"I slipped it under the door of the trailer, when no one was around. That way anyone could have done it. I wasn't thinking about blackmail, and definitely not murder. Really! I just wanted them to know that someone knew about it, that they couldn't keep it a secret. I just wanted them to tell the truth! That's all! I just wanted them to tell the truth!"

She collapsed into louder sobs. Detective Figueroa spoke quietly, gently.

"I can understand that, Lucy. You just wanted them to be honest."

She nodded as she continued to sob. "But they wouldn't. I think Hannah might have, if it was up to her, but Nina said no. When they had that first conversation about it, Nina said no. She said no one would find out, and they should just keep it quiet, and that wasn't right! They had to tell the truth!"

"But they didn't."

"No! The note only made it worse! Nina said the way to defend themselves was to keep it quiet. She said the note meant blackmail, and they should just pay."

"But that wasn't what you meant."

"No! I swear! It wasn't! But, I mean, if they were already planning to pay someone..."

"Then why not you?"

"Aren't you supposed to do that? I mean you always hear you should take advantage of opportunities. That's just being smart."

"So you arranged a meeting."

"I left another note. It said to bring ten thousand dollars or the truth would get out. I hadn't planned that. Really! It was them! I didn't even think of it until I heard Nina talk about blackmail!"

"Why Olvera Street?"

"I don't know. It seemed, I mean, I didn't know where to pick, and everyone working on the film was always talking about it, and it's a place everyone knows. I don't know. I had to pick someplace."

"So you chose a time."

"3am. I thought nobody would be there then, and I was right. It was quiet. I got there really early, just a little after 2, and I hid. I didn't know if anyone would show up. I said come alone, and just leave the money in this one trash can. I'd seen that in a movie, they left the money in a trash can. I didn't know how to do this kind of thing. I'm not a criminal! But I didn't know if anything would happen, so I just hid and waited. I didn't really expect to get the money. I swear! I thought no one would show up, or maybe they'd come with the police, and I would just run away, and not even try to get the money."

Lucy grabbed another tissue as a fresh rush of tears erupted.

"But she, she was there early too, and she must have seen me hide, followed me, or something. She, somehow she found me, and she attacked me! I mean it! She hit me first! It was self-defense! I was just protecting myself!"

"Hannah found you, where you were hiding?"

"It was self-defense!"

"And then while you two were fighting, she fell, and she hit her head on the edge of that stone step."

"I'm not a murderer! I just wanted them to tell the truth!"

The detective placed a fresh legal pad in front of her and handed her a pen. "I understand that, Lucy. I understand it all now. All you have to do is write it down, everything you just told me, everything that happened. Just write it all down."

She started writing as she continued sobbing. "It's just not fair. None of it is fair." She grabbed another tissue and blew her nose, but that just seemed to bring on bigger sobs. "I was willing to work hard for it. I really was!" She blew her nose again, and this time it seemed to calm her a little. "I just wanted my chance. I was going to be an executive producer."

CHAPTER 23

Mutual Admiration

Now that the case was solved, I went to Detective Figueroa's office downtown to get my official form signed and submitted. As intrinsically satisfying as it is to help with murder cases, I won't waste a chance to get paid for it.

It was an overcast morning, so the room wasn't as bright as I remembered, and there weren't many people there, so it was relatively quiet. I handed my form to the detective, and he signed it without even looking at it, except to make sure he wrote on the correct line.

"Don't you want to read it over first?"

"Why? Did you make any mistakes filling it out?"

"No."

"Did you claim any hours when you weren't actually working on this case?"

"No."

"Then it's correct, right?"

"Yes."

"So I don't need to read it over."

"I don't think you're supposed to just trust me to fill it out correctly."

"But I do. I'll bet you were extremely careful about recording your hours."

"I was, but…"

"And I'll bet you double and triple and quadruple checked it for accuracy."

"I did, but still…"

"If it's really important to you, I'll read it over."

"I think you should."

He spent five or six seconds looking up and down the page, and then handed it to me.

"It's perfect, Ella."

"Thanks, Joe. I'm not sure you read it very carefully, but I'll take it."

"I do want to say thank you. I couldn't have closed this case without you. You were a great partner."

"I appreciate that, Joe. I enjoyed working with you."

"I wasn't sure, when Mac recommended you. I mean, you know he's a very honest guy, and when he told me about you, he said, you know, full disclosure, he told me you two were dating."

I tried to keep from giving any indication of shock, but according the the new look of concern that appeared on the detective's face, I was not succeeding.

"That's okay, right? That he told me that? I don't mean to make you uncomfortable. Maybe I should have told you before."

"It's all right. It's fine."

"He told me that, but he said you worked together before that, and that you did a great job. I mean, that wasn't why he recommended you. He just, like I said, and like I'm sure you know, he's an honest guy, and he's always going to disclose something like that."

"Yes."

"I only mentioned it because I wanted to say that you really did excellent work. Mac was right. I would recommend you too."

"Thank you."

"Maybe I shouldn't have said anything."

"No, Joe. It's absolutely fine. You just took me by surprise a little. I appreciate the compliment." It wasn't the content of what he said that had unnerved me. It was just that one word. "Dating" sounded so serious and official. It hadn't occurred to me to characterize it that way.

Detective Figueroa still looked worried. I felt the need to prove that everything was all right.

"And I need to return the compliment, as well. You are an excellent detective, and I am glad I got the chance to work with you."

That did seem to calm him a bit.

"Well thank you, Ella. I appreciate your saying so."

"So, I suppose I give this form to an administrator? To whichever person here is the equivalent of Melanie Browning?"

"Melanie Browning! Is she still there?"

"You know her?"

He laughed. "Melanie Browning? That's who did your initial paperwork, got you signed up as a consultant?"

"Yes."

He laughed again. I waited for him to elaborate, but it didn't seem he was going to.

"Is there a problem with Melanie Browning?"

"Well, no. I mean, I'm sure your paperwork is fine. She wouldn't, I mean, I'm sure she does her job well."

"Then why was that your reaction to hearing her name?"

"Oh it's nothing, I mean, nothing important. Oh man, I am not doing well today. Just sticking my foot in it right and left. I'm sorry."

"I don't understand."

"It's nothing, really. It was all so long ago. I was just surprised that she would have stayed there this long. I didn't realize, and Mac didn't mention, but why would he? I mean, why would it matter? Probably it's all ancient history now anyway. I mean, I don't think she would still, I mean, no."

I waited a few seconds to make sure he was finished talking.

"So, where do I hand in my form?"

"I'm sorry, Ella. It was really nothing. Years ago, Mac and Melanie went out on one or two dates, maybe three, and it didn't work out, and that was all there was to it, except..."

"You don't have to tell me."

"Except she really liked him. She carried a torch, for a long time, but I'm sure she's over all that now."

"It's really none of my business."

"It's nothing. If it was anything, Mac would have said something."

"It's fine, Joe."

"I'm sorry. I just can't stop my mouth today."

When I was finally able to convince him that he hadn't done any damage, and that I was perfectly fine, he guided me to the correct administrator's office, where a skinny bald man wearing a bolo tie took my form and put it in a file. The detective and I said our goodbyes, and I headed to the parking lot.

On the drive home, I thought about the suitability of the word "dating" and determined that it did actually fit the situation. I had been momentarily surprised by it, but it was just a perfectly accurate descriptor, nothing of any more import than that.

As for Melanie Browning, it seemed Detective Figueroa had expected me to be upset, perhaps jealous, because of his revelation, but I wasn't. I had long ago guessed that there must be some sort of history there, and from what Joe said, it didn't amount to much. Whatever intentions Ms. Browning might be harboring didn't concern me at all.

CHAPTER 24

The Chao Family

Lucy Moss would be going to prison, her dreams of an influential Hollywood career shattered. According to Aunt Louisa, Lucy's aunt Julia was trying a variety of tactics to reduce, if not remove, the embarrassment to the Moss family, sometimes claiming Lucy's confession was coerced, and sometimes that her actions were the result of some vaguely defined condition that could be solved with a stint in rehab. So far, Julia wasn't getting much support in her endeavor.

I was glad the Chao family would at least know what had happened to Hannah. Surprisingly, the one of them who appeared in my thoughts most often was June Chao. Maybe it was because she had supplied such important information for the case, or maybe because I felt a little sorry for her, stuck in her bedroom with her oxygen mask. I decided to pay her a visit.

Ordinarily I would call first. I don't much like it when people show up at my house uninvited, so I don't like to inflict that experience on others, but I remembered how excited Matilda the housekeeper was to entertain visitors, and how much June had wanted to talk. Despite certain people's recent criticisms, I still think formality has its place, but so does spontaneity.

Matilda seemed startled when she opened the door, and the first thing she said was, "Oh my!" I started to think my abandonment of formality had been a mistake.

"We sure are having visitors today!"

"I'm sorry to arrive unexpectedly. I can come some other time."

"No! No! No! Come in! Come in! Mrs. Chao will be so happy!"

Matilda actually grabbed my hand and pulled me inside.

"It's practically a party now! First her son and her daughter-in-law, and then her granddaughter, and now you."

"I don't want to intrude on the family."

"Don't be silly! Right this way."

She led me back to the bedroom, knocked on the double doors, and then opened them without waiting for any response.

June Chao was in the bed with her oxygen mask, as expected. Arranged around her in a variety of different kinds of chairs were Edward and Christina Chao and their daughter Olivia. All four of them had their eyes trained on a large television mounted on the wall. Matilda started to announce my presence but was cut off by an assortment of dismissive gestures and "sh" sounds. I then received four welcoming nods, and June pointed at Matilda and then at another chair, along the wall. Matilda picked it up and placed it in a spot near the bed, but not blocking anybody's view. It seemed I was expected to sit there, so I did.

The focus of the family's attention, on the television, was Nina Chao, who was sitting next to Oscar winner Stephanie Warrick in front of a giant poster that said "Sterling" in big letters, underneath a picture of Ms. Warrick's face. The two women were being interviewed by an entertainment reporter whose face I recognized but whose name I didn't remember.

"It must be so difficult, Nina, to be able to concentrate on giving a good performance, when so many difficult things have been happening."

"Yes, you're right. It has been very challenging. I'm just so lucky to have someone like Stephanie here, to give me advice and encouragement. She's been so amazing through everything." She turned a worshipful gaze toward Stephanie, who sent back a warm smile.

"I've only done what anyone would do in the circumstances. Nina has been going through so much. I just try to help in any small way I can."

"She's been incredible. I never could have kept going without her help."

Stephanie smiled again. "She doesn't really need it. She is so strong, and so talented! She's doing great work on the film."

The reporter turned from Stephanie back toward Nina. "Well that's quite the compliment. What do you think about that, Nina?"

"Oh my god, Stephanie Warrick just said I'm talented. I will remember this day for the rest of my life!"

At that the tape of the interview ended, and instead we saw the entertainment reporter, whose name, I finally remembered, was Rory Templeton, back in the studio, talking to the host of the show.

"Wow, Rory. Nina Chao is showing amazing resilience!"

"She really is, Ashlee. It's been just one tragedy after another for her. Her sister was murdered, by her assistant, of all people, and meanwhile, her agent was arrested for embezzlement. It really is a case of truth is stranger than fiction!"

"It is, Rory, but she's coping so well. She must be a very strong person."

"Absolutely, but you know, Ashlee, she is lucky to have Stephanie Warrick by her side."

I noticed movement on the bed, and turned to see June Chao moving her hands around on the duvet, apparently looking for something.

"She really is, Rory. Once again we see how generous Stephanie is. It's true what they say. She is the nicest person in Hollywood."

"It's so true, Ashlee. It's just wonderful to see that, and I can't wait to see this film!"

The television went black and silent, and I saw that what June Chao had been looking for had been the remote control.

Christina Chao was dabbing at her eyes the same way she had when I had last seen her, at her house, but this time with a yellow handkerchief rather than a blue one. Then I heard her speak for the first time. Her voice was soft and melodic. "I didn't know Nina was friends with Stephanie Warrick."

Olivia laughed. "She's not, Mom. That was probably the first time she said more than three words to Nina."

"Are you sure?"

"Yes." It seemed Olivia did not want to discuss the subject further, because she turned abruptly to me. "Did you have some loose ends you need to tie up?"

"No. I came because I wanted to thank your grandmother for her help. I'd like to thank all of you, actually, for answering all those intrusive questions. We couldn't have solved the case otherwise, but especially you, Mrs. Chao."

"June."

"All right, June. Thank you especially."

She took a long breath from her oxygen mask, while everyone else in the room waited expectantly, but all she finally said was, "You're welcome."

With the television no longer providing a focal point, the room became quiet except for sporadic bursts of awkward conversation. After about ten minutes I figured I could politely take my leave, and I met no resistance. Matilda saw me to the door and insisted that I come back anytime. I thought I might. I suspected June had plenty of interesting things to say, when her family wasn't around.

I turned on the radio for the drive home, mostly to listen to the traffic report, but it was all full of the murder and the movie, especially how it affected Nina. I heard about the rumor that she and Anthony Kells were involved in a real life romance. I heard that there was already Oscar buzz about Stephanie Warrick and her costar Jack Laraby. I heard a number of comments about the many tribulations of Nina Chao, and how well she was managing them. I didn't hear Hannah's name at all.

CHAPTER 25

Grandfather

Grandfather Graepenteck's favorite place in the world was a cabin in the tiny mountain town of Tall Fir Creek, near Big Bear. The community of Tall Fir Creek considered themselves diehard mountain folk. None of them rented out their houses to tourists, and they all lived there right through the winter, even though they sometimes got snowed in. In his later years, his son (my father) and his sisters (Aunt Agatha and Aunt Louisa) used to try to convince him to move someplace warmer, or at least to spend the winters with one of them, but he wouldn't budge. He often said, when I visited him there, that it was where he belonged, and nothing would ever convince him to leave.

I called him Grandfather, not out of any desire for formality, on either of our parts, but because there was a brief period, when I was very small, when I was obsessed with Johanna Spyri's *Heidi*. He wasn't Swiss, but he lived in a cabin on a mountain, and even spoke German, so I started calling him Grandfather, and he loved it. He never gave in to my entreaties to buy a couple of goats, but he did indulge me with mountain hikes and picnics consisting only of huge hunks of bread and cheese. He taught me some German too, although all I can remember now is how to count to ten. The name Grandfather, however, stuck, and I called him that for the rest of his life.

The little golden bicycle wouldn't have had so much significance if it weren't for the timing. Grandfather was always giving me presents, and he'd given me other things from Germany, and other things his father had given him. It was the fact that it was the last thing he ever gave me, and that neither of us knew, at the time, that it would be. He was old, when he died, but in good health. His end came suddenly, due to an aneurysm. He quite literally dropped dead, right there in the cabin, his favorite place in the world.

I told Cormac Roth about all of that. We were sitting on my overstuffed grass green sofa, and he had his arm around me. It felt nice, comfortable, right.

"I was close to my grandfather too, my mother's father."

"The one who was a policeman?"

"Yeah, from a long line of Chicago Irish cops."

"And your grandmother was actually from Ireland, near Dublin, right?"

"A little north of Dublin, yeah. He met her in the war. We called him Pop."

"And you wanted to be like him."

"Yeah, my dad wasn't happy about that."

"You didn't tell me that part."

"He liked Pop well enough, he just thought his own career was a couple of steps up from police work."

"Tax law?"

"Going to an office in a suit and tie, not dealing with violence and crime. He couldn't understand why I'd want to spend my time looking for criminals instead of coming to work with him. I spent the first three years of college avoiding telling him I didn't want to go to law school. Luckily my brother is more like him. After Declan passed the bar, Dad eased up on me. I guess he felt better knowing one of us was doing the smart thing."

"I don't know. I think you have to be pretty smart to do what you do."

"You think so?"

"Definitely."

"Hey, Ella?"

"Yes?"

"We've been seeing each other for a while now."

"Mmhm."

"And it's going well. At least, I think it is."

"Sure. Yes. I think so too."

"Good. So, maybe we should, I mean, I think we should, you know, make it official."

"Official how?"

"Be exclusive, you know, official."

"Oh. Okay. Um, sure. I guess so. I mean, yes, all right."

"Are you sure? If you don't want to, if you think it's too fast..."

"No, I want to. I just, I mean, I'm surprised. That's all."

Suddenly I felt my heart beating fast and my face getting red. I tried taking a deep breath, but it didn't help. I stood up.

"Are you okay?"

"I, uh, I need to get some air."

"What's wrong?"

"I'm fine, or I will be. I just need to take a walk."

"But it's late. It's dark. It could be dangerous."

"I'll be fine. I just need a few minutes. I'll be right back."

"Ella!"

I couldn't stop myself. I felt a desperate need to be outside. As soon as I'd closed the door behind me I started to feel a little better, but I still felt I had to keep moving, so I just started walking down the sidewalk, toward the beach.

It was very quiet. I could hear every step I took, and the regular rhythm of that sound helped my heart rate and my breathing slow, and after a while I was able to stop moving and to take a look around me.

It seemed as if I had been outside only a few minutes, but I was one block away from the beach. I had walked more than twenty blocks. Since I'd come that far, I decided to go all the way. I walked over to the beach, took off my shoes, and dug my feet into the cold sand. I walked until I found a spot just short of the high water line, and then I sat there facing the ocean. Soon I felt calmer, almost back to myself again.

Sunrise over a west facing beach is a gentle thing. In California, sunsets are the ones with the drama, the bright circles dropping into the sea. If you're staring at the ocean in the early morning, the sky just gradually lightens, first grey, then different shades of blue, maybe a little pink coloring the clouds, if there are any. The water lightens too, equally gradually. Everything slowly shifts from night to day, with no clear line dividing the two. It's the best time to be there, before anyone but the waves and the birds is there to distract from the peace of it. It always raises my mood.

I was feeling fully calmed and relaxed, about to get up and go home, when I heard the faint swish of someone walking through the thick, dry sand behind me. It seemed like an optimum moment to leave, and there was the possibility that whoever it was would be dangerous, so in one movement, I stood up, turned around, and picked up my shoes, ready to use them as weapons if necessary.

It was Cormac.

My shock must have been obvious, because the first thing he said was, "Sorry. I didn't mean to sneak up on you."

"It's all right. You did, sneak up on me, I mean, but I'm the one who should apologize."

"I didn't want to yell from far back there, to disturb you, interrupt you. I was about to say something."

"To announce your presence."

"But you stood up."

"I heard you walking."

"You have sensitive hearing."

"I suppose so."

We stood there staring at each other for a minute or two, me holding my shoes, him wearing his, but holding something in his right hand that I only gradually noticed. Before I asked him about that, though, I had another question.

"How did you know I was here?"

"I didn't. I went looking for you."

"But what made you think to look here?"

"You said early morning was your favorite time to come to the beach."

It wasn't a satisfactory answer, but I accepted it anyway, and moved on to a higher priority question.

"What's that? In your hand."

He looked down at his right hand as if he had forgotten it was there.

"I found this, after you left. I saw something sticking out from under the couch. I thought it was a spider at first, but it was this."

He opened his hand to reveal something golden, and not at all like a spider.

It was my grandfather's little bicycle.

I reached out, slowly, and took it. I was looking only at it, but I could feel him still looking intently at me.

"It was under the sofa? But I looked there."

"I think it had been stuck behind the leg. I must have knocked it out. I sort of kicked the leg when I stood up, and there it was."

"Thank you."

"I'm glad I could help."

I lifted my head up to meet his eyes.

"I'm sorry, Mac. I don't know what happened. Something..."

"It's okay."

"It's not. It was rude of me, and weird, and I'm really sorry."

"Are you all right now?"

"Yes. It won't happen again. At least I don't think so."

A seagull cawed, the waves tumbled and thrashed against the sand, and we turned our backs to the ocean and squinted into the rising sun.

Thank you for reading *The Executive Producers*! If you enjoyed it, or even if you didn't, please post a review wherever you read reviews, and share your opinion with the world.

Someone at this very moment is trying to decide whether or not to buy this book, and a review from you could help that person immensely.

Please visit esteigerandco.com if you would like to know more about author Erika Maren Steiger and her other books.

Acknowledgements

I feel immense gratitude to everyone who helped me complete this third book in the Ella Graepenteck series, including fans of the first two who were kind enough to provide a wide variety of suggestions. I would particularly like to thank Paul E. Steiger, my father, for continuing to impart his writing and editing wisdom, and JoAnn McKenna, my mother, for supporting me in so many ways. I am especially grateful to my amazing friend Kimberly Kalaja who, despite being immersed in a year of intense stress and severe losses, insisted on helping me anyway. I am very lucky to have such people in my life.

Books By Erika Maren Steiger

Ella Graepenteck Genealogy Mysteries:

The Moving Pictures

The Leading Ladies

The Executive Producers

Other Books:

Floating on Bamboo